PRAISE FOR THE ROYAL ACADEMY REBELS SERIES

"*Misfits* is funny, charming, and rebellious…just like Devin. I can't wait to see what happens next!"

—James Riley, *New York Times* bestselling author of the Story Thieves series and the Revenge of Magic series

"Calonita, author of the Fairy Tale Reform School series, twists familiar stories around once again in this series starter, which places a plucky heroine in the ever-popular boarding school setting. A cliff-hanger ending will leave readers eagerly awaiting the next installment."

—*Booklist*

Also by Jen Calonita

Fairy Tale Reform School
Flunked

Charmed

Tricked

Switched

Wished

Cursed

Royal Academy Rebels
Misfits

Outlaws

Heroes

ROYAL ACADEMY
REBELS

HEROES

JEN CALONITA

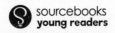

sourcebooks
young readers

Published by Sourcebooks Young Readers, an imprint of Sourcebooks Kids
P.O. Box 4410, Naperville, Illinois 60567-4410
(630) 961-3900
sourcebookskids.com

Library of Congress Cataloging-in-Publication data is on file with the publisher.

Source of Production: Sheridan Books, Chelsea, Michigan, United States of America
Date of Production: August 2021
Run Number: 5022537

Printed and bound in the United States of America.
SB 10 9 8 7 6 5 4 3 2 1

For Lindsay Currie, who always knows exactly what to say

Happily Ever After Scrolls

Brought to You by FairyWeb—Enchantasia's
Number One News Source

Royal Academy: The Revolution!

by Sasha Briarwood

Buckle up, royal watchers! It's me, Sasha Briarwood (yes, Princess Rose's way cooler younger sis). Thanks to this snazzy new column *Happily Ever After Scrolls* gave me, I am the one who gets to tell you all the happenings with Royal Academy and its young pupils.

And who better to tell you about young nobles than a young noble herself?

So let's start with this juicy tidbit: My name has been cleared!

Followers of *HEAS* know that Royal Academy's former headmistress Olivina came gunning for me and my friends Raina and Heathcliff White (Snow's siblings), along with Devin

Nile and Logan Nederlander, after she decided we weren't behaving "royally" enough to be allowed to stay at Royal Academy. The truth? She didn't like that our sleuthing had uncovered the truth about her rise to power. Olivina is responsible for some of the biggest princess mishaps our kingdom has ever seen!

Snow's sleeping death? Olivina! Rose's long nap? Olivina! Princess Ella's hellish housekeeper years? Olivina! Determined to keep royals in check, Olivina has been grooming the latest princes and princesses at RA in outdated practices meant to keep us all under her thumb.

Once my friends and I shared the truth about Olivina with the world—with help from other ousted RA kids whose identities have been kept private—the headmistress had no choice but to flee the school and (hopefully) never return! Don't fret. The Dwarf Police Squad is currently hunting her, as well as Enchantasia villains Rumpelstiltskin and the wicked fairy Alva, who have also been causing so much trouble of late. (I mean, how batty does a villain have to be to want to cast a curse that erases the history of our kingdom? I'm hearing that's what Rumpelstiltskin and Alva are trying to do. My sources tell me they'll all be apprehended before this scroll even magically appears on your parchment!)

I, however, am going nowhere. You'll find me celebrating at an upcoming Royal Academy bash in my friends' and my honor. And there is much to sprinkle pixie dust about. Royal Academy has a fresh new view and new co-headmasters—Princess Snow and Professor Pierce (a former royal and a current teacher at the school). I'll be sharing updates as I have them, but for now, let's party like it's the end of the Troll War! There is nothing but glass slippers and fancy balls on the horizon.

◇◇◇◇◇◇◇

For more on the search for Olivina, Rumpelstiltskin, and Alva, continue reading Happily Ever After Scrolls*!*

REIGN ON ME

If you'd told me two weeks ago that I'd soon find myself back in the Royal Academy headmasters' office wearing an itchy ball gown, I'd have said you were bewitched and would have thrown my uncomfortable glass slippers at your head.

But here we are.

And it makes no more sense to me now than it did at the start of this all-important meeting requested by Headmistress Snow (White) that I'm attending with my friends, our parents, and an entirely too-perky new fairy public-relations liaison.

"This is *so* exciting! Isn't this exciting?" Emerson Emet is fluttering around the room in a shimmery electric-green dress that leaves glitter in her wake. "It's a new dawn at Royal Academy, and you all get to experience it together!"

My proud parents are sitting alongside Snow and my favorite teacher, Professor Pierce, who is now co-headmaster of the school. The rest of my friends and their families are here too, sitting on settees around the newly redecorated headmaster's office (which was all but destroyed during our showdown with the fairy godmother a few weeks ago). Gone is the wall of mirrors that Olivina secretly used to spy on her students. Her oversize desk covered with multiple maps of the kingdom (that she used to hunt down her granddaughter, Tara) has been taken away as evidence by the Dwarf Police Squad. Her faithful assistant, Hazel Crooksen, hasn't been seen since the night we turned Olivina's mirrors on her and broadcast the truth about her wickedness to everyone at her party. But instead of being worried about where Olivina or Hazel are, apparently the new headmasters have called us into this office to plan…a party.

"*I'm* excited!" Emerson adds, her green eyes bright as she zooms in front of my face. "It's not every day a group of formerly banished Royal Academy students gets reinstated and given a royal court commendation scroll for bravery!" Emerson tosses glitter into the air. "Let's give it up for our courageous students!" She waves her wand in the air, and tiny fireworks come flying out.

The assembled parents and teachers applaud. My friend Logan, who is allergic to pretty much everything but air, starts to cough from the smoke. His mother pats him on the back.

"And look! Even our royal court is cheering for you today!" Emerson taps a mirror on the wall and we see a live shot of the royal court. Princesses Ella, Rapunzel, and Rose are waving to us from halfway across the kingdom. The missing member of their reigning quartet is Snow, who serves double duty as an RA teacher and now headmistress (and also happens to be the older sister of two of the formerly banished—Heath and Raina).

I feel someone poke me in my back. "Smile, Devinaria!" my mother hisses. "Princess Ella is looking at you!" Mother dabs at her eyes with an embroidered Royal Academy hand-kerchief, which was included in the gift basket the royal court apparently gives all subjects who receive commendations. (Also included: Rapunzel's hair-care products, rose-scented perfume, and our own mini-glass-slipper paperweight that says, "Live Like There's No Midnight.") I suspect my mother is taking all of my gifts home with her, which is fine by me. Can I go home with her too?

Emerson stops cheering, and the fireworks and glitter dissolve into thin air. Her smile goes from sweet to deadly serious. "Sadly, all celebrations must come to an end." She taps the mirror with her wand and the waving princesses disappear. "Now it's time for us to get to work." She flies around the room, stopping at each student. "You've helped rid this kingdom of a dangerous villain and proven you are true leaders who can change with the times. That is why the royal court feels you are the face of this new royal revolution, as Sasha is calling it in her new *Happily Ever After Scrolls* column. The kingdom is under a great deal of stress with the hunt for the villains Rumpelstiltskin and Alva and now Olivina. We need to take the attention off the villains and put it on you brave, young heroes." She waves her wand and glittery words appear on a pale-pink wall.

Operation Royal Refresher!

"Heroes?" Logan squeaks. "Does that mean you want us to hunt Olivina down, because one second she was here and then *poof!* She was gone." He blots his brown forehead with the handkerchief tucked into his new RA chef's jacket. "Which means she could be anywhere right now…including here."

"Oh, Logan, don't be ridiculous," booms his father, a tall, broad man who's said to secretly be part of an elite force of dragon hunters. (Dragons that Logan has long claimed to be allergic to.) "Olivina wouldn't be foolish enough to stick around Enchantasia with a bounty on her head. She's long gone." His eyes narrow. "But she will be caught, I can tell you that. As will Rumpelstiltskin."

"Oh, yes, please catch Rumpelstiltskin!" agrees Sasha's mother, looking around at the other parents as she places her teacup on her saucer on the table. "Have you heard the rumors about him and the wicked fairy Alva? They want to create a curse to rewrite the history of our kingdom!"

"Nonsense! A curse like that can't be done!" argues my father, looking regal in his royal guard jacket with its dozen or so medals dangling off the right side of the sash. "That's just another rumor put out by the media. You can't rewrite time!"

"They say he has almost all the ingredients he needs to erase the history of our kingdom and rewrite a new one where he's in charge," Logan whispers, looking terrified. "Stiltskin brought Alva back to life! If he can do that, he can certainly cast a rewriting curse with the most powerful fairy our kingdom has ever seen."

"Yeah, but those kids at Fairy Tale Reform School—like Gilly Cobbler—are out of school and going after the final ingredients to stop him," says Sasha.

Sasha's dad looks at her pointedly. "Where did you hear that?"

"*Dad*," Sasha says with an eye roll. "Reporter, remember? I have sources everywhere—including at FTRS. Cobbler's crew is tough. They can take him."

"I hope so," says my other roommate, Raina, who is wearing a glittery silver ball gown and a tiara as if she's headed to a coronation. "Otherwise all this talk of giving Royal Academy a public relations makeover is going to be short lived. In a week, we could be erased."

The room is quiet for a moment.

"Rumors spread lies!" Logan's dad declares. "We shouldn't give this curse another thought. There is no way Rumpelstiltskin will make it happen."

All of the parents and guardians start talking at once. I

haven't given this villain talk much thought since we got back from the forest. My friends and I look at one another and shake our heads. Royal-magic politics. Another thing I have little interest in. Give me a squirrel with a nut allergy who needs dietary advice over this any day.

How did a reluctant princess who has only ever wanted to be a creature caretaker become a poster child for a royal revolution? That's what I want to know.

Schooling at Royal Academy was never on my wish list, but after I got my "invitation" (which should really be called a "sentence" since it's mandatory), suddenly my life was all about following backward royal protocols and staying in a wicked fairy godmother's good graces so that I wouldn't be banished from my kingdom. But banished we were, tossed out into the woods where my friends and I had to figure out how to clear our names with the help of fellow royal vigilantes like Robin Hood and Red Riding Hood (no relation) and other expelled students like Olivina's secret granddaughter, Tara.

I look over at the quiet girl in the corner of the room. Her dark amber legs hang over the arm of the chair as she lounges sideways and plays with one of the six braids woven into her hair. She's the only one of us not in a ball gown since she hasn't officially agreed to attend RA yet. Instead, she's in a casual red romper. I still can't decide if I know Tara any better today than I did a few weeks ago when we met, but I can tell she looks as thrilled to be in this meeting as I do. Who can blame her? At least the rest of us have family here. Tara's only family was the grandmother she tried to hide from so she wouldn't be raised evil.

"What do you think, Devinaria?" asks the perky fairy, fluttering in front of the velvet armchair I'm sitting on. "Are you up for the challenge?"

I stare at Royal Academy's shiny new public-relations director (hired by our kingdom's reigning princesses) and wonder what challenge I'm supposed to be answering the battle cry for. Fighting for the rights of all students to have the chance to lead their kingdom? Leading the hunt to find Olivina and bring the fairy godmother to justice? Suggesting the school come up with a better uniform than one that involves petticoats and ball gowns? "I'm sorry, could you repeat the question?"

Emerson's green dress glitters as she swoops over the room and taps her wand against the pink wall again. New words appear.

*Step One: It's a new royal day! Let's do our
part and show the kingdom all is okay!*

"The royal court wants you all to be spokespeople for the kingdom! We have Sasha writing about the changes coming to this school in *Happily Ever After Scrolls*. Raina has graciously agreed to take carriage rides through the countryside to see subjects nervous about letting their children apply to RA. Heath will hold public forums where he can assuage parents' fears and assure them this school is up to the task of safely molding today's youth. Logan will teach cooking lessons via magical scroll, proving that young royals can be more than just figureheads; we have chefs! And"—she looks at a boy with charcoal eye shadow who is wearing a killer black silk dress shirt—"royals who can change the course of dialogue through theatrical productions, like the one Corden is going to put on about the fall of Olivina." She turns to a girl with red hair and a glittery face seated next to Corden. "And we have Prue to thank for the high-tech mirror inventions being used to teach the Dwarf Police Squad how to hunt villains. You're turning your once-tragic banishment into something this kingdom can embrace and cherish! You are Enchantasia's new hope!"

The parents in the room toast us with their fizzy drinks (triple-checked by Prue in case Olivina is still hanging around and trying to poison us).

"The only two I haven't received a plan from are you and Tara," Emerson says to me, her smile waning slightly. "But when I saw you in the hall yesterday, you swore you had a great idea that you'd announce today."

I laugh lightly. "I did say that, didn't I?"

My headmasters stare at me encouragingly. The other parents are watching me.

"Uh…" Drooping dragons, I've been caught off guard. Again. "I…"

Yes, Sasha has been writing blog posts all week and Raina has been cramming for this meeting since we were invited three days ago, but I've been sort of busy. When word got out that I was back in the castle, every mouse in the castle walls came calling for my services. I've been so busy mixing cough syrup, plucking herbs for sinus infections, and teaching a nervous flying squirrel how to fly again that I've had no time to figure out how I can contribute to this royal hogwash. I just want to do my caretaker work and be left alone. But that clearly won't fly with everyone in this room. "I…"

"Devin?" Emerson prompts. "You *do* have a suggestion, don't you?"

"I..." I'm sweating. *Help. Someone help me. I need a diversion!*

And that's when something large falls from the ceiling and lands on Snow's desk, causing everyone in the room to scream.

BEST-LAID PLANS

People in the room dive away from Snow's desk as I rush over and pick the offending item up.

"Lily!" I cry, hugging my bearded dragon to my chest. "I haven't seen you in two days! Have you been out in the woods? What's going on out there?" She's grown so much of late that she's the size of a poodle now. Mother says Lily should be on a leash so she doesn't wander off, but that's just offensive. Lily is her own creature! If she wants to stick with me, she'll stay, and she does. She just likes to get out on her own now and then to get fresh air. I wish I could too.

Sasha's mother looks aghast. "You know that thing?"

"It's her pet bearded dragon, Mother," Sasha explains. "Meet Lily."

"Does she have to always make an entrance like that, dropping out of the ceiling or falling from chandeliers?" my mother asks wearily.

"Lily likes to be original," I say, putting her down on the desk and feeding her a cricket I've had saved in a tissue in my pocket for when she returned. Lily flicks her tongue in excitement and sucks the cricket in. Then she flicks her tongue at me again.

I've got an idea for you: say you're going to talk to the animals about Olivina's whereabouts!

That's a great idea! "I'm going on a mission to talk to our most important assets in the kingdom!"

Emerson's eyes sparkle. "You are? Who are they?"

"The animals, of course," I say and my mother groans.

"You just want to work on that creature-care thing you do!" Mother says and looks at my father. "I thought she grew out of this already."

"Dear, she has a talent," my father says, looking embarrassed that our family is choosing to have a squabble in front of other royals. "Can we hear her out, please?"

"Thank you, Father," I say brightly. "I was thinking I could address the woodland creatures in the kingdom and let them know they haven't been forgotten." I pull at the itchy ballgown wishing more than anything I was wearing comfortable pants right now. "If villains are on the loose, we'll need the animals' help in tracking them. If I can convince our creatures we are their friends, not foes, I can get them to keep us posted on any sign of trouble. Of course, convincing moose and bears to join our forces could take time," I add hastily. "Maybe I could stay out there indefinitely and report back in a month or so?"

"You want to go alone?" Mother cries. "But you're a princess! Princesses don't travel alone! You need an escort!"

"She could come with me."

I look up. *Enchantasia Insider*'s Most Eligible Prince, Heathcliff White, is smirking at me.

"The parents *I'm* meeting with about RA are all in very remote places—the kind of places Devin needs to go—so we could go on this diplomatic mission together. I'll talk to the people and she'll talk to the creatures." His blue eyes are playful.

Diplomatic mission. *Please*. If I know him, that sketch pad he's taking "notes" on is probably full of ideas on how to ditch his itinerary and go troll hunting. That's fine. He can hunt trolls, and I can search for yeti to help. "Works for me!" I tell the group.

Mother narrows her eyes. She knows what I'm thinking.

"Traveling with the prince sounds wonderful, but can't you just stick to talking to humans?"

"Mother, caretaking is my gift and I want to use it. I'm convinced it's why Olivina wanted me at RA in the first place." I look at the others. "She probably thought she could get me to make the animals of this kingdom rise up against the people."

"Could they really do that?" Logan asks, concerned.

"They'd never," I promise, "but it would help if someone let them know we're on the same side. Caring for creatures, and learning how to do it well, is something I'm good at." I look at my parents again. "It's all I've wanted to do since I realized I could converse with the spider that was nesting in my windowsill." I look at Emerson. "Isn't helping them doing my royal duty?"

"Hmm…" Emerson taps her chin. "I guess, but animals aren't going to talk to the press and we need some good publicity." She frowns.

"Are you saying animals' lives aren't as important as our own?" I feel myself starting to wind up like a top, preparing a big speech I clearly haven't rehearsed. Lily flicks her tongue as if to say *Bring it!*

Snow clears her throat and steps in, swishing over to my side in a yellow gown with several layers of crinoline underneath. "Emerson is *not* saying that. You are clearly a talented emerging creature caretaker, Devin, but right now we really need help with our human subjects. They are frightened after what happened with Olivina, and now with this Rumpelstiltskin business, they're even more so. We need them to know we have things under control."

"I have an idea," Headmaster Pierce speaks up. "What if we have Miss Nile teach a mini magical scroll course on creature care from inside the castle? She could teach others around the kingdom basic ways to care for their pets or creatures in need, and they could tune in by mini magical scroll."

"Oh, that's a splendid idea!" Snow says.

"Yes!" Emerson has her wand scribble some notes on a scroll. "I love it! We can get *HEAS* to cover it as well."

Snow looks at me. "What do you say, Devin?"

It's not the same as being out there on the grounds doing there on the grounds doing real work, but it's something. My mother clears her throat. "Thank you, that would be lovely," I say automatically. *Lovely* isn't exactly the word I'd use, but...

"What a bunch of warts!"

I turn around. Tara's face is as red as her romper. "My grandmother is on the loose, and instead of putting all our resources into catching her and these other villains she could be in cahoots with, you want us to hang around here doing busy work to make royals look good?" The room is silent. "This place is hogwash just like it was the first time I came through these doors! It's all smoke and mirrors!"

"Tara, I understand you're upset about your grand-mother," Snow says gently.

"No, you don't! None of you understand what my grand-mother is truly capable of! If you did, the only thing you'd care about right now is finding her!" She races out of the room and slams the doors behind her.

"I'll go after her," Pierce says. "Excuse me."

"My, my, that one *cannot* speak at our royal banquet, that's for sure." Emerson tut-tuts. "Which reminds me... Please have your ball gowns and dresswear ready for inspec-tion before the ball tomorrow evening. I want to make sure you coordinate but don't clash or, fairy be, all wear the same color." She shakes her head and more glitter emerges.

"Now might not be the best time to mention I haven't picked out a dress."

"You'll all be expected to say a few words to your fellow students and subjects about how you're ready to come to

Enchantasia's aid now when we need you the most." She waves her wand at her notes on the wall, and her scrolls disappear. "On that note, let's disperse. I need to get to the Royal Underground for a Charmiccino."

All the parents and my friends make their way out of the room talking about magical coffee drinks and shoe choices for tomorrow night, but Tara is right. Why are we playing games when villains are on the loose? I stand there, wondering what I'm doing back in this room, in this castle, in these clothes.

The room is quiet. I pull a pamphlet out of my dress skirt pocket and stare at it again. On the cover is a picture of a dragon, a hedgehog, a wild boar, and a unicorn with a young girl smiling as she stands beside the creatures. I try to imagine what it would be like to be that girl and read the description on the pamphlet again.

Nottingham School for Nature and Wild Beasts

Training the kingdom's best creature
caretakers and animal whisperers since the
Troll War. Classes for grades six and up!
Enroll now!

I open the pamphlet and look at all the courses. They teach everything from herbal medicine to holistic care and have classes on difficult creatures, mythical and magical creatures, and even bugs. The school is located in a remote mountaintop village in Nottingham, which is only a few hours from Enchantasia. Isn't that where Robin Hood is from? And he's in Enchantasia all the time.

"Devin? Are you okay?"

I turn around. Snow is watching me. "Oh, I didn't realize anyone was still here."

"I am sorry for the way that meeting just went," Snow says. "I know you wanted more than we're offering, and I know you're desperate to get out and work with animals. We'll get there." She sighs. "We're just spread so thin at the moment. We have to focus on one thing at a time, and assuring the people that we've got things under control and restructuring this royal program are our number one priorities. I hope you can understand." She glances down at my hand. "What do we have here?"

I try to stuff the pamphlet back in my pocket. "Oh, it's, uh…"

She takes the pamphlet from me and studies it for a

moment. "Nottingham…oh." She looks at me again. "This is a good school for creature care. I've heard wonderful things."

"Have you?" I ask excitedly. "I found this pamphlet in my room on my bed and…"

"In your room?" Snow's smile fades. "You don't know who gave it to you?"

"I thought maybe you did, but…"

"It wasn't me," she said gently. "So I think we should check the pamphlet for hexes. Who knows if someone is trying to persuade you to leave for a reason?"

"They don't have to push hard," I say with a sigh.

Snow puts an arm around me. "Don't fear, Devin. You're going to love the new Royal Academy. I promise you. You belong here. I can feel it, and soon you will too."

I watch Snow place the pamphlet on the desk behind her. I don't want to be impolite and tell the princess she's wrong, but my gut tells me I belong anywhere but here.

CHARMICCINOS CURE EVERYTHING

There's our favorite animal whisperer!" Heath calls out as I storm out of the headmasters' office with Lily on my heels.

Raina, Sasha, Heath, Logan, Prue, and Corden come running up to me, the girls' heels clicking on the marble floor. Logan gets sandwiched between my roommates' too-large skirts. Staring at them in their royal finest—dresses dotted with rhinestones with large hoop skirts, and jackets covered with Royal Academy sashes—I'm struck by how much they "look" like they belong here. Why do I still feel like I don't?

"So what were you talking to Snow about after we left?" Sasha prods, and I notice her notebook and pen hovering in the air behind her. The girl is always in reporter mode.

"She didn't ask you to give a speech on our behalf tomorrow night, did she?" Raina's brown eyes are full of worry. "Because she said we could all speak, and as her sister, I kind of feel like if only one of us is allowed to speak, it should be me."

"Your coloring does work well in candlelit situations." Corden lifts her chin to the light of the nearby stained glass. "And if I charm the dress you're wearing one more time, the blue will practically glitter."

Raina squeals and claps her hands. "Yes! And you'll do my makeup too?" Corden nods. "And *only* my makeup? I really want to stand out since we're being honored. Princess Rule 25: Why blend in when you're meant to stand out?"

"Why are you still reading the *Royal Academy Rules* book?" Sasha groans. "Olivina is gone! Throw that rule book out! Snow and Pierce aren't going to use it."

"I can't help it!" Raina says with a sigh. "Some habits are hard to break."

I slip off the heels I was wearing and pull my boots out of the bag I brought with me. *Aaah*…much better. "Did you guys see Tara when you got out here?"

"No, she was already long gone," Corden says grimly.

"I'm sure she hasn't fled the premises or anything, but it's better to leave her alone when she gets like this."

"We don't want to spook her," Prue agrees. "She hasn't even agreed to re-enroll at RA yet. Just let her cool off."

"I think it's pretty cool the headmasters are letting her stay here while she decides," adds Corden. "RA is definitely the safest place for her to be right now."

"Are you sure we shouldn't talk to her?" I try again. Tara was so upset. "Because Tara running away while Olivina is on the loose is *not* a good idea."

Prue and Corden look at each other. "No, we're sure," says Corden. "She knows she's better off here than anywhere else. Just let her be."

A clock chimes somewhere in the castle, the sound low and sharp like a foghorn.

"That's my cue," says Prue. She taps the mini magical scroll in her hands, and I notice there's an antenna sticking out of it along with a crank and several flashing silver and gold buttons. "Headmistress Snow is letting me run security protocol with the Dwarf Police Squad for tomorrow night's party. I've rewired Milo the Magic Mirror to be on high alert throughout the castle. Watch." Her glittery face lights up as she taps a few things on the scroll, She turns the crank, and the mirrors in the hallway light up gold.

"Welcome to Royal Academy Security 3000!" booms Milo, who I must say sounds much more chipper than normal.

"Whoa," Logan says.

Prue pulls Logan to her side. "It's best if you all stand right next to me, especially you, Heath," Prue says. "Step away from the mirror. Quick!" We cram around her and I hold Lily.

"Please state your name and your reason for being in the headmaster's wing," Milo says pleasantly.

Prue puts her fingers to her lips.

"I'm sorry," Milo says. "I can't hear you."

"Very polite," Logan whispers and we all shush him.

"I will ask you one more time." There is a hint of warning in his voice. "If you cannot provide a valid reason for your appearance, then"—lights in the hallway flash and flames erupt from the lanterns nearby—"to the dungeons you go!" The floor drops out a few feet from where we're standing.

A pixie flying down the hallway shrieks and flutters away.

"I knew we had a dungeon here somewhere!" Sasha shouts excitedly as Raina clings to her arm.

Prue punches a few buttons on the scroll again, and the

lighting returns to normal as the floor slides back into place. "You should see what happens if someone tries to enter the dormitory. The whole staircase gives way!" She grins with glee.

"Uh, that's great." Heath runs a hand through his blond hair. "One problem: What if you're eating a turkey leg and your mouth is full or you're trying to hide from a pack of lovesick princesses and you can't answer Milo?"

"I'm sorry." I immediately bristle. "Are you saying any girl who wants to talk to you is a lovesick princess?"

Heath shrugs. "Well, if the glass slipper fits." Raina, Sasha, Prue, and I freak.

"What if they just need to borrow a quill?" I ask.

"Or they want to tell you that there is gum on your shoe?" Sasha seconds.

"Or they're trying to find out the class assignment for Is That Edible or Poison?" Raina wonders aloud. "Are you saying you're just going to hide from them and let Milo send these princesses plummeting to their death?" We all glare at him.

"They're not falling to their death; they're falling to the dungeon." Heath is still missing the point.

Prue frowns. "Hmm...maybe you guys are right. We

might need a time delay for answers. I was really hoping to catch Olivina with this thing. I even added her signature scent along with Hazel Crooksen's vocal recognition so Milo won't miss them, but I guess there *are* some kinks to work out." She hits a button and Milo's mirrors go dark again. "I should probably talk this over with Pete Stubridge, the Dwarf Police Squad chief. We have a meeting in a bit."

"You can't move the meeting to later? I thought we were going to the Royal Underground today," Corden complains. "I never got to go my first time here because I was banished after three days. I'm dying to go to Little Miss Muffin's and meet Marta Marigold."

"Oh, you'll love her," Raina says. "Royal Academy's royal dressmaker is a genius, but maybe a little less so now that I've seen your designs. She'll probably want to snatch you up as a designer."

Corden beams. "You think so? Then forget Charmiccinos! I want to go to Marta's!"

"What's a Charmiccino?" I ask.

"It's the signature drink served at that new coffee shop, Charmed, I'm Sure," Sasha explains. "They opened while we were banished. Everyone at RA is obsessed. I had one yesterday for my blog post. They're sweet and creamy, and they taste like whatever you want them to."

"What do you mean?" Corden asks.

"I mean, after they make it, you say what you want it to taste like—like a caramel chocolate-fudge or apple pie—and it does!" Sasha shakes her head. "I can't figure out how it works."

"I'm dying to dissect the recipe," Logan chimes in. "If it's that good, maybe I can make one for my father and he'll stop asking me to join his dragon-hunting crew. He thinks now that I've fought a firebird and a wicked fairy godmother, I'm ready to fight a dragon." He sneezes. "Even though just the thought of those things makes me... *Achoo!*"

"Blessed be!" Sasha says. "And get this—the drink changes colors as you drink it depending on your mood! There is even a star cookie on the top that you crack open to reveal your fortune. Yesterday mine was spot-on."

Lily and I look at each other. *No way that works*, she says with a flick of her tongue.

I agree. "What did your cookie tell you?"

"It said the night of my life was upon me." Sasha gets a swoony look on her face. "Obviously, it refers to our commendation at tomorrow night's ball."

"*Obviously*," Heath and I say at the same time.

"I should really go," Prue says again, and we all groan. "Don't worry, I'm leaving you with a parting gift!" She fires up her magical scroll again, cranks the side three times, then presses the gold button four times, and a new portrait of Pierce and Snow as headmasters pops open to reveal a hole in the wall. "This slide will lead you straight to Charmed, I'm Sure. You'll slide out right around the corner behind a lemon tree."

We all *ooooh*.

Sasha steps up to the swinging portrait and hops in. "Meet you down—*there!*" Her voice echoes as she slips away.

Raina goes right after her, followed by Corden and then Logan, who surprisingly doesn't even try to get out of going.

"Coming?" Heath asks, and I wonder for a moment.

Will a Charmiccino fix everything?

Snow took my Nottingham School for Nature and Wild Beasts brochure. She dismissed the idea of me even wanting to go there. She thinks someone might be hexing me and wants me to stay here to learn a modern royal way of life. Yes, being here is better than banishment in a tree house in the woods, but no matter how hard I try, I still feel restless.

"Lily? What do you think? Should we go?" I ask my pet.

I don't do slides, she says, and meanders back down the hall. I'm sure she's headed to our dorm room, but the thought of sitting in there and daydreaming about a school I can't go to sounds depressing.

"Lily's out, but I'll come with you," I tell Heath.

He winks. "I thought you might. Race you down!" he shouts and swings himself into the opening.

I climb into the portrait and push off. I can see Heath ahead of me, a scream escaping his lips as he whips around the first darkened corner. He's gaining speed while I can feel my heavy skirt slowing me down. I grab hold of the skirts and bunch them up, pulling them tight around me. I start to descend again, moving faster and faster till I fly out of the slide and land on a settee conveniently placed behind the lemon tree. The others are waiting. Logan is plucking leaves out of his hair.

"I came out of the tube too fast and crashed," he explains.

"Can we get Snow to turn all staircases into slides, please?" I ask. "That was fun."

"Let's go," Sasha says. "I've got free Charmiccino passes for us, thanks to my post yesterday, and that line can get long." She steps out from behind the lemon tree and into the Royal Underground.

Royal Academy's shopping mecca for students is packed. There's a crowd near the dress shop where Marta works and lines at Little Miss Muffin's and Pattycake Bakersman's food mart where people usually go to get dorm room snacks. I can see a few kids window-shopping at the fencing equipment and school supply store, while others are hanging out and doing homework at tables and chairs in the courtyard, under a bewitched magical ceiling that changes its weather depending on its mood.

Today, the ceiling is bright blue and there are no clouds in sight. I see a huge line underneath a glittery sign that says CHARMED, I'M SURE. The sign keeps blinking as we approach. The shop is different from the others in the Underground. The walls are painted with a silvery glitter that is almost blinding, and the tables and chairs all appear to be made of glass. I can hear the sound of milkshake concoctions being blended from several shops away and several people laughing and talking as the line slowly moves.

I start counting heads and pause. "Sasha! There are thirty people in line!"

"No," Sasha says, not making eye contact as she gets in line behind everyone. "It's more like ten."

"No it's not. Look!" I motion to the pixies, fairies, trolls, and humans ahead of me. *Wait a minute—trolls and fairies? Huh. That's new.* Usually the only people who could access the Royal Underground were RA students, and RA students had to be human, which means... "Wait. Did Snow and Professor Pierce change the admission policy for attendance at RA?"

"Yes!" Sasha says, linking arms with me. "And I'll tell you all about it while we wait in line." I start to protest. "It will move quickly. I promise. Yesterday I only had to wait thirty-five minutes."

"*Thirty-five minutes?* For a frozen drink?" I protest. "Nothing can taste good enough to wait in this line. Nothing!" I hear a scream and stop talking.

Two girls, one dark-skinned, one a fairy who is bright blue, have just emerged from the shop carrying ice-blue and silver shakes. One girl's shake is still sparkling; the other's has fizzed out but is starting to glow and pulse. *BAM!* A baby unicorn appears at the girl's side, wearing a pink Charmed, I'm Sure bandanna around its neck.

The blue fairy squeals louder and throws her arms around the unicorn. "My wish was granted! I got a unicorn!"

Everyone in line starts to applaud. The second girl blows out her sparkler on the shake and a second unicorn appears. People start jumping up and down and applauding as the girls lead the unicorns away.

"These are more than just drinks," Sasha tells us. "They're experiences. See what you'd miss if you didn't go to school here?"

I try to think of a clever response.

"Don't answer that," Heath warns me.

"Come on, Devin! You belong here with us," Logan says. "I know RA was never your dream, but Snow is really trying to make things better. Look at what she's doing with opening admission to nonroyals and changing the course curriculum."

"Don't you want to stick around and take Beyond the Magic of the Mirror: What's the Real Role of Royals?" Raina asks.

"Or Pretty Lethal: Learning How to Save Yourself?" Heath asks. "It's part of the new martial arts and fencing program."

"I'm excited for Mad as a Hatter: Fashion's Role in How the Kingdom Sees Royals," adds Corden.

"And Wicked Good: Changing the Apple Stigma," Logan pipes up. "We're learning all kinds of apple recipes!"

"Plus, there's Reigning Right: The Power of the People, one called There's No 'I' in Rule, and even something called Kingdom Creatures: They're More Than Just Sidekicks. You'll love that one," Sasha says. "I just hope they have enough teachers to run all the classes."

"What do you mean?" Prue asks.

Sasha leans in conspiratorially. "My sources tell me some of the teachers are spooked by all the villain uprisings. The royal court is doing what they can to assure everyone they're safe at RA, but no one will feel safe till the villains are caught."

"Tell me about it," Raina says with a deep sigh. "Olivina is out there somewhere, and it's only a matter of time before she returns to seek revenge."

We're all quiet for a moment. Then more squeals from the Charmiccino line distract us. I watch as a short-haired girl wishes to have red hair extensions and a boy grows apparently two inches in front of our eyes. ("The effects are temporary," Sasha says. "No wish lasts forever.")

"I, for one, am not scared of Olivina," I say, returning

to our conversation. "And all the new classes *do* sound great. It's just…"

I can't put my finger on what's still bothering me. Maybe it's the idea of being groomed to lead a kingdom when all I want is to work with my hands helping animals in need. Or maybe it's that I've never craved the spotlight like my roommates do. And part of being royal means being in the spotlight. We've been in it enough during our first few months at school to last me two lifetimes. But as Sasha and the others look at me earnestly, I know that's not what they want to hear.

"I'm sure I just need to get used to all the changes," I say instead, and I let the conversation turn to something else. Logan's take on the Little Miss Muffin shop's best muffin is such a long conversation ("Blueberry versus rhubarb? Who could decide?") that we make it to the front of the line before he's finished.

Several fairies are hard at work mixing drinks and taking orders when I reach the counter. A few others are decorating the finished shakes with little trinkets and sparklers.

"Name?" a fairy in a flashing Charmed shirt asks.

Sasha pokes me in the side. "Devin."

"Chocolate or vanilla base?" the fairy asks, not looking up from her notepad.

"Vanilla?" I guess. "Oh, and I'd love to add some chocolate—"

The fairy cuts me off. "The Charmiccino knows what your heart desires. It will be in there. *Next!*"

Sasha ushers me down the line, and we watch as a series of brown or white shakes are quickly created and topped with mini muffins, doughnuts, a toy tiara, and sparklers. I pay a crazy amount for my shake, then accept it from the final fairy.

"Make a wish!" she squeaks as I take the cup.

A wish…

I hear screams of delight ahead of me. Raina is wearing a coronation gown as a crown is placed atop her head. "I'm queen!" she calls to me as Logan winds up in a full chef ensemble with an embroidered name tag that says OFFICIAL ROYAL COURT BAKER. "I have always wanted this job!" he says with a laugh.

BOOM! There is a cloud of smoke and people scatter as a shake explodes and drops black ash all over the floor. The kid holding the shake is also covered in black soot.

"What happened?" I ask.

"He must have wished for something outlandish or inappropriate, and the Charmiccino wouldn't even consider it," Sasha explains. "When that happens, the shake explodes. So wish wisely." She blows out her sparkler. "I wish to run the largest scroll news source in the kingdom!" *POOF!* A long piece of parchment with the words ENCHANTASIA INSIDER written across the top appears in Sasha's hands. "Look! My blog has gone worldwide! I knew it would happen someday." She runs off to show the others.

Heath appears by my side holding a sparkling milkshake that has turned royal blue. Mine keeps changing colors. One minute it's green. The next it's yellow. Finally it's powder blue, then it morphs into pink, then it starts to change again.

"So, what are you wishing for?" Heath asks.

I stall. "What are *you* wishing for?"

He blows out the sparkler and looks at me. "Nothing." He shrugs. "I'm a simple prince. I already have all I need." I give him a look. "I'm not into the showy display of wishes, okay?" He takes a sip. "But these taste too good to deny myself so I drink them, not wish upon them. What about you?"

I already have all I need. I sigh. I don't feel the same way, and Heath is one of the few people I can share that with.

"I wish that exposing Olivina didn't mean I had to come back to Royal Academy," I blurt out. "I wish it meant that I could go to the right school for me, which seems to be Nottingham's wild creature school. It's not that I don't want to be with you guys. I've just always had a plan. Long before I was forced to go to RA, I wanted to be a creature caretaker, and I feel like at Nottingham I'd get the classes I need to become the best ever." I'm getting excited now and can't help myself. "And then maybe once I'm trained, I can train more kids who want to be caretakers, and I can form an alliance and we can spread out throughout the kingdom and maybe I can open a proper caretaker clinic and… Well, the shake isn't going to do all that so I'm not wishing either." I blow out the sparkler and the drink turns a putrid brown. I think it's mad at me.

"Wow, you've got a lot riding on one wish." Heath shakes his head. "I don't know why you fight this so hard."

"Fight what?" I ask as I take a sip. Oh! It tastes like chocolate syrup and apple pie. Yum. The Charmiccino really is good.

"Being royal," Heath points out. "You can't walk away from it, so why keep trying? Embrace it! Enjoy the finer points, like having a Royal Underground, going to a cool school, having progressive teachers and a group of friends that are the envy of all." He flashes me his best smile. "We are out of banishment, and we're the talk of this school and the kingdom. This is your moment. Take it and worry about your future later."

"I guess," I say, but inwardly I can't help but wonder: What if who I want to be and who the royal world wants me to be never line up?

ROYAL ACADEMY

A message from Headmasters Snow White and Pierce

All students are welcome to attend the commendation ceremony for our brave, reinstated students who fought valiantly in the face of villainy.

Day: Friday evening

Time: 4:00 p.m.

Place: Royal Academy Ballroom

Attire: It's a new dawn at RA, so the dress code* is nonexistent and completely up to you!

◇◇◇◇◇◇◇

*Although dress of some kind is required.
Let's not get out of control here.

CHANGE IS COMING

P in? Sticker? Sash?" The girl at the door thrusts the items in our faces. I notice something different about the banquet hall room right away—and not just because there is a new banner hanging across a wall that says ALL ARE WELCOME HERE. The swag the girl is holding and even the student holding it is different. This girl is an ogre wearing a pantsuit! To a ball!

"Thank you! Oh wow, this is the new Royal Academy logo?" Sasha asks, taking a pin and pinning it to her dress.

"Yes, it is!" says the girl, showing off her silver sash which has the RA insignia and a new tagline—ROYAL IS A STATE OF MIND.

"Cool," I admit as I take a sash and place it over my head.

"Have a seat anywhere you want," the girl says. "There

are no seating charts anymore *or* waiter service. We're having a buffet."

"No. Way." Logan's eyes go wide as he spies the long tables around the room where there are platters of roasted meats, jiggly desserts, and the biggest fruit basket I've ever seen.

Gone are the overdone candelabras and decorations that usually dominated Royal Academy events. Instead there are simple sprigs of wildflowers on each wooden table, and benches have replaced uncomfortable chairs. Students are mingling, wearing everything from simple frocks to casual jackets and shirts. I don't see many tiaras or glass slippers. Instead, I see girls in boots similar to the ones I'm sporting under my lilac dress paired with pants. I'm happy to see everyone took the headmasters' invitation to heart and dressed the way they want. Raina is still wearing a gown, of course, but that's Raina, while Sasha looks fairy-tale chic in a knee-length gown that swishes when she moves. Even the boys are in their daywear, rather than decorated suits.

I'm sad Lily isn't here to see this. She opted out of the festivities after the debacle at the meeting yesterday. She's currently lounging in my dorm room, enjoying a feast of crickets.

"Should we take a table over by the food?" Logan asks, not waiting for an answer. "I'm starving!"

We follow him to a table, weaving through the crowd on the dance floor. The one thing that has stayed the same is the entertainment. Gnome-More is playing again. I'm surprised they're back. Between the harpy incident and Olivina's wrath at our last event, I wouldn't think they'd be caught within a hundred miles of this castle, but there they are.

"Miss! Miss!"

I turn around. My former lady-in-waiting, Brynn Haun, is rushing toward me. Gone are her uniform and the cap that hid her dirty-blond hair. She's wearing a pretty silver gown with a crystal bow, and her hair is in loose curls. Her brown eyes are warm as she grabs my hands. Right away, I notice she's wearing one of the new Royal Academy sashes.

"Brynn! You're officially a student?" I say in surprise.

"Yes, miss!" She flushes with excitement. "Headmistress Snow officially enrolled me this morning. I'm one of the school's first nonroyal students. I passed the entrance exam with flying colors," Brynn adds proudly. "She said I know more about what it means to be royal than most royals."

"Well, I could have told her that!" I hug her. I know this is something Brynn has wanted since I met her, but since her royal heritage is practically nonexistent, prior rules wouldn't allow it.

"Do I look all right?" she asks, spinning around for me to admire her dress.

If anyone looks the part of a royal (and is even more so one on the inside), it's Brynn. "You look perfect, Brynn. Really." I am about to ask what her dorm room number is—we could easily fit another bed in our room—when I hear my name being called.

"Devinaria! Devinaria!"

I cringe. It's Emerson, half flying, half walking over to me. Her arms are full of papers. She takes one look at me and frowns.

"Pants? I…"

"We were told we could wear anything we wanted tonight," I remind her.

"Yes, but…" Her lower lip curls down. "I just thought you'd dress more like this lovely young royal here." Her smile returns. "How have we not met yet? I'm Emerson Emet, and I'm…"

"Oh, Brynn isn't royal," I interrupt, enjoying myself. "She's RA's first nonroyal student."

"Oh." Emerson's smile waffles. "Well, that's just lovely!" She turns back to me. "What I really need is a royal's help right now. We have some out-of-town kingdom reporters here covering your return to RA and the changes to our fine school, and I was hoping you would give them a quick interview. What do you say?"

"That sounds fun, miss. I mean, *Devin*!" Brynn pipes up. "You can tell them all about our new school motto—Royal Is a State of Mind."

"Well, maybe don't mention that," Emerson says quickly. "I'm not sure it's official yet. Some of the students decorating got ahead of themselves. Just speak very royally about how everything in Enchantasia will be fine, nothing to fear, we're stronger than villains, yada, yada, sparkle, sparkle, you get the idea. And smile a lot."

Emerson sprays something in my face, and I start to cough.

"There. Now you smell like lilies. Reporters love lilies! It's said to be a soothing scent that will put them in a good mood."

I give Brynn a quick wave before Emerson escorts me to a corner of the ballroom where I see two ogres with scrolls and self-writing quills interviewing several students. Emerson is jabbering away about them—how influential they are, what I should be saying and not saying (don't utter the words *Olivina* or *Rumpelstiltskin*), but I'm not exactly paying attention. Not when I see who they're interviewing. It's none other than Clarissa Hartwith, the most loathsome princess in this school. She's wearing an intricate silver gown with a skirt so large, I'm afraid she's going to knock over a table.

"I really don't understand what all the pomp and circumstance is for," I hear Clarissa saying. "Why are we rewarding students who didn't follow the *Royal Academy Rules* book?"

The ogress in a black silk dress looks perplexed. "Because the students exposed your headmistress as a villain, which means they did the right thing. Don't you agree?"

"I guess." Clarissa sniffs. "Personally, I find traditional royal ways appealing. The word 'royal' means we have a pedigree that makes us worthy of being leaders. The fairy-tale world has worked this way forever. Why do things have to change? My parents are considering moving our family to a new kingdom where there are schools that follow royal protocol. Royal Academy has clearly gone downhill."

"Do you want to pull the ribbons out of her hair or should I?"

I spin around, expecting to see Emerson, but she's nowhere to be found. Instead, Sasha is standing behind me looking as angry as I feel.

I hold out my arm, thankful to have my roommate at my side. "We'll do it together."

"Clarissa?" I call sweetly. "Don't you think you should get going? Midnight will be here before you know it and we don't want everyone here seeing you turn back into a toad." Sasha snorts.

"Is that true?" asks the ogre, scribbling notes furiously.

"No, it's not true!" Clarissa snaps. "This girl is a trouble-maker! She's the reason the school is failing!"

"Me?" I'm outraged. "You're the troublemaker!"

"I'm not the one who brought Olivina's granddaughter back to the school when she clearly wanted no part of it," Clarissa seethes. "Can't you see she doesn't fit in here?"

"Tara was as wronged by Olivina, as we all were," Sasha fires back.

Clarissa puts a slim, pale hand on her right hip. "If that's so, where is she tonight? I haven't seen her walk in to accept her heaps of praise from our *acting* headmasters."

Sasha and I briefly look at each other.

"She would have gladly accepted praise," I counter, eyeing the reporter, "but she wasn't feeling well so she stayed in the room." Believe me, we all tried to convince her to come, but all she wanted to do was sleep. "She has a bad headache."

Clarissa purses her pink lips. "Of course she does. Convenient excuse if we wind up getting attacked tonight."

"We're getting attacked?" the ogre squeaks. "Where did you hear this?"

"She didn't hear it anywhere," Sasha says. "She's making it up."

"Princess Rule 26: Beware of big events," Clarissa recites from the Royal Academy Rulebook. "They are the perfect place for a villain to attack."

My nostrils flare. "Tara is not a villain. Olivina is."

Clarissa smiles. "Are you sure about that?"

"Uh, guys? I don't think we're supposed to mention Olivina," Raina says, smiling tightly as she approaches. "Hello again, Evan."

"Raina." The ogre nods. "Great interview earlier."

"Thanks," she says, and touches her hair. "I thought it went well too."

I glare at Raina. "We're kind of in the middle of something here."

"*Yes*," Clarissa adds. "You already had your interview. This is mine, and I want to talk about how suspicious Tara is."

I laugh. "And why do you think Tara is suspicious?"

"She doesn't smile and she's always wearing her hair in multiple braids," Clarissa says to Evan, who is scribbling furiously.

"What does that have to do with anything?" Sasha complains.

"I fear for my safety with her in the school with us," Clarissa continues. "If you ask me, Olivina is innocent and Tara is the one who should be questioned about all the mishaps in this kingdom. That girl clearly wanted to frame her grandmother."

My blood is boiling over, like one of Prue's spell concoctions. "You're just spreading lies," I seethe. "Why don't you do us all a favor and stop threatening to leave the kingdom and actually LEAVE!" I don't realize till it's too late that the music has stopped. I've just shouted my thoughts to the whole ballroom.

What can I say? I know how to yell. How else can I call out to the animals of the forest?

Headmaster Pierce swoops in. He looks dashing in a gold suit and one of the new Royal Academy sashes. "Hello again, Evan," he says. "I'm sorry, but perhaps we should conduct this interview after Headmistress Snow speaks."

"Of course," Evan says and snaps his fingers. His quill stops writing and jumps into his jacket pocket.

Pierce turns to the rest of us. "Students, I need to speak to Devin for a moment, but Clarissa don't go far," he adds as he leads me away. "Enjoy the roast duck. It's delicious!"

I sniff. "I hope there is a vegetarian option."

Headmaster Pierce gives me a pointed look as he leads me off to the side. I have a perfect view of the ballroom doors where some of the kingdom's elite are still streaming in. I haven't spotted my parents yet, but they must be here by now.

"What was going on back there?" he asks.

"Clarissa started it!" I protest.

"Devin, I—"

"I know what you're going to say," I cut in. "This wasn't the time or place."

He gives me a look. "That was part of my speech, yes."

"And I need to just play my part and help the kingdom get back on its feet," I add, growing even more frustrated.

"No," Pierce says, surprising me. "I was going to say, 'I'm sorry.'" I raise an eyebrow. "I know coming back to RA was never your intention. Clear your name, yes. Be a spokesperson, never. And now that you're here, we've asked you to take on a bigger role than you wanted. I apologize for that." Pierce smiles sadly.

My mouth is open so wide I fear I could catch flies. "So does this mean I don't have to do any of the stuff Emerson wanted?"

"I'm afraid I can't get you out of that," he says kindly. "You're part of the package—the royals who exposed the headmistress—and I'm afraid the spotlight is clearly on your head. Not what you wanted to hear, I know."

"I just want to focus on creature care and be left out of all this other stuff," I say with a sigh. Around us, students are laughing and smiling. The *Happily Ever After Scrolls* sketch artist is doing a portrait of Corden and Prue. They look completely comfortable with the spotlight. I've never been, and I don't know how to change that.

He nods. "Being royal comes with a lot of baggage and expectations."

"Is that why you didn't take your title back?" I wonder. "Now that Olivina is gone, you could have been a prince again, couldn't you?"

He hesitates and I notice him looking over at Prue and Corden. "We discussed it, Snow and I, but in the end, I still don't want the title."

"Why not?" I ask, unable to hide my curiosity.

"Because I don't like how the title weighs me down with its specific path." I notice his voice becoming tense. "When I let Olivina strip my title that day so long ago, my life changed. It was frightening at first, but I grew to love my new role of ushering students into the future monarchy and helping them figure out who they are. I realized I was good at it. I've taught so many students to be tolerant, inclusive, and to think of the world at large, rather than just their kingdom. And I've done it all without a title hanging over my head."

"So why do *I* have to be pinned down by a crown?" I argue.

"Because it is still the way our kingdom operates, I'm afraid," he says. "My title was taken away, but you have one. That means you must follow the royal path. For now. Not forever." He stops me from interrupting. "Creature caretaking isn't going anywhere, Devin. If that's truly your dream, and I suspect it is, you'll find a way to make it happen. Just not at this exact moment. Does that make sense?"

"Yes," I say. "I'm just tired of waiting. I want things to change now."

"I know," Pierce says, putting a hand on my shoulder. "Give it time."

"Good afternoon, Royal Academy!"

I hear Snow's voice and look up. The headmistress is standing on the dais while the rest of the royal court—Princess Rapunzel, Ella and Rose—are beamed in behind her via mirror. Heath motions to me to make my way to the front of the room, but I feel weird walking away from Headmaster Pierce.

"I'm so excited to talk to you this afternoon about Royal Academy's makeover," Snow begins. "While changes to a royal way of being are almost unheard of, these were inspired by the recent actions of some truly brave students—both royals *and* nonroyals. Their courage, selflessness, and kindness got us thinking. Why does a crown decide who is worthy of ruling? Shouldn't our leaders include anyone who truly wants to do good in this kingdom?" A cheer rises up from me and my friends, and Snow smiles. "The answer is yes, and that is why Royal Academy has gone through some changes that the royal court has approved wholeheartedly. No longer will this school only accept royal students. We are opening our doors to applications from all students—human, fairy, ogre, troll, and otherwise!—who possess these characteristics and truly have the urge to help make a greater Enchantasia."

I look over at Brynn, who is beaming, and I've never been more proud. This is the way Royal Academy should run, and I can't help being impressed by our royal court and Snow who made the changes so quickly after Olivina's ousting. Brynn is the princess I've never been, and I can't wait to see what she does now that she's an official student.

"Royal is no longer just a title," Snow continues. "It's a state of mind! We're excited for all of you to embrace this thinking with us and…and…" Snow grips the podium and appears to take a few gulping breaths. Something is wrong.

"I feel so strange…" Snow grabs her head. She looks out at the audience and her eyes land on Headmaster Pierce. "Pierce, I… Something's…" Snow collapses, and there is a collective gasp. Heath and Raina go running toward her. A siren wails and Milo's voice rocks the room.

"Royal Academy Security 3000 activated! Danger! Danger! Danger!"

Prue comes racing by me with her mini magical scroll, punching buttons.

I grab her arm. "What's happening?"

"I don't know," Prue says. "It's not a glitch. Something is happening and… Oh my stars. Look at the royal court!"

I glance at the mirrors again and see Ella and Rapunzel doubled over while Rose frantically tries to figure out what is happening. Suddenly both princesses vanish. Students in our ballroom start to scream.

"Look at Snow!" someone cries.

Headmaster Pierce, Heath, and Raina have reached her, but her whole body waffles and disappears in their arms.

"Students of Royal Academy!" Princess Rose addresses us from the mirror. "I'm afraid Rumpelstiltskin has managed to cast his curse and is trying to rewrite the history of our kingdom!" People in our ballroom cry out in terror. "The other princesses have already disappeared, and I don't know how much time I have left to guide you. Run, students! Run while you can! Get to Fairy Tale Reform School. I pray the former villains can keep you safe there! Run!"

"How is she still here, then?" Brynn asks, breathing hard next to me. "She's a princess too!"

"Yeah, but Rose has flirted with the dark side. Maybe she's immune to this curse," I say, trying to stay calm as we hear a loud boom in the distance, followed quickly by another one. People in the ballroom rush toward the door, but I can't leave without my roommates. Where are they?

Logan appears at my side with Corden. He's hyperventilating. "We have to get out of here! If Princess Rose is correct, Rumpelstiltskin might be coming and will try to make us all disappear!"

"That's impossible, right?" Sasha asks, running up behind him and looking at me. "My sources said a curse of this magnitude could only happen during a Fire Moon. Those only occur every few decades!"

I rack my brain trying to remember what else I know about this curse from *Happily Ever After Scrolls* and Sasha's blog posts. Truth be told, I've been kind of busy trying to out a villainous fairy godmother. Maybe I should have paid more attention to what was going on in my kingdom. Another rumble makes the ground beneath us shake.

"We've got to get out of here," Corden says. "Where's Prue? Has anyone seen Raina?"

"Raina!" I shout, my heart fluttering so fast I feel like it's about to leap from my chest. I get bumped from behind and knocked into Logan. People running past are going to trample us. "Heath!" I shout. "Prue!" But it's no use. Everyone is a blur.

"Run, students! Run! Get to Fairy Tale Reform School!" I hear Rose shouting from the mirrors as Milo's siren continues to wail. "Get to—" The mirrors go dark. The lights flicker in the ballroom and people scream.

There is another loud boom and I hear a crash. Portraits are falling off walls. People are knocking over tables to get out, and the china place settings and goblets are falling and smashing into a thousand pieces.

"We have to get out of here!" Logan yells, grabbing my arm.

The ogre reporters bang into us on their quest to get out the door. "We're under attack!" one shouts.

"Not without Heath, Raina, and Prue," I say, jumping onto the nearest chair to see if I can get a better vantage point. The dais they were on is now empty. And Lily! I have to get back to my dorm room and find Lily! "I don't see them. I—"

"Devin!"

I hear my name being called from afar. Heath has Raina and Prue with him and is racing toward us.

"There they are!" Sasha cries as the ground shakes again. The fighting outside the castle seems to be getting closer.

I jump off my chair, ready to grab their hands and run for it. They've almost reached us when—*BOOM!*

The entire ballroom seems to shift as debris rains down on our heads, forcing us to dive for a still-standing table and duck underneath. There is screaming and crying and lots of smoke. We're all coughing and covering our mouths, but I can see Heath, Raina, and Sasha through the haze, but they've made it under the table. Raina is in hysterics about Snow, but they're okay. We're okay. For the moment. But what is happening? Where has the royal court disappeared to? Are our whole lives about to disintegrate in front of our eyes? We have to get to Fairy Tale Reform School. If Rose is right, it might be our final chance. I inch out from under the table.

Heath grabs my arm. "What are you doing? Stay down!"

"I need to see what is going on!" I cry, wrestling my arm away.

The two of us peek out from under the table. There is a thick layer of smoke, but the air is eerily quiet. I look up. Through the haze, I see a massive hole giving us a perfect view of a smoky, bright-red sky and a fire-red moon. There is only one explanation for what's happening.

Rumpelstiltskin's curse is here.

Happily Ever After Scrolls

Brought to You by FairyWeb—Enchantasia's
Number One News Source

Special Edition: Surviving the Curse—What's Next for Enchantasia?

by Sasha Briarwood

If you've come to my column looking for the refreshing wit you expect from my blogs, today's post may be a letdown. How can I be witty and light when we all almost died last week?

It's been ten days since Enchantasia was nearly wiped from existence by Rumpelstiltskin and Alva's curse. The battle is finally over, but it will take a long time for our kingdom to recover. It's been ten days since any of us have felt normal. Ten days since we've felt safe. The kingdom we know is not gone, but it is going to take a while to get back to normal. And what is normal anyway? It's like… Forget it. You don't need another blogger going off on some long-winded rant. (To the magical bloggers guilty of this, you know who you are!) You need information post-curse. You need answers, and I'm here to tell you what I know from the royal perspective.

With Rumpelstiltskin's curse stopped, the royal court is once again safe. Princesses Ella, Rapunzel, Snow, and Rose have been returned to us and are all being held at a secure location. They are working tirelessly to get the kingdom up and running again. Princess Ella even gave my sister a statement for me to share with all of you: "Never fear, Enchantasia. Our kingdom will rebuild and thrive once more. The villains have been done away with and can't hurt you. We will emerge stronger than ever. Have faith!"

Thanks to a group of fairies and Fairy Tale Reform School students, led by the legendary Gilly Cobbler (that former pickpocket seems to be a part of every major villain battle this kingdom has seen the last few years), Rumpelstiltskin and Alva have been banished. While there were countless injuries and damage kingdom-wide, the greatest destruction was to Fairy Tale Reform School.

The ELF Construction Company is working tirelessly to get the school up and running again, but every part of it must be checked for jinxes, hexes, and countercurses before it can be rebuilt, which means "a lot of red tape," as one anonymous ELF crew member told me. What red tape is, I'm not sure. I'm told it's scroll variances and paperwork. Boring! Rumor has it those students are going to have to be housed somewhere in the interim. The question is where?

The good news is Royal Academy itself was untouched! Well, except for the ballroom, but with all that's going on, who has time for balls? There has already been a ten-day halt on classes, during which all us students have been held indoors at the Royal Underground beneath school. When are we heading back to class? This week or never? I know, I know, lucky us. (Still hoping my plea to delay the start of magical midterms for another month will be heard.)

◇◇◇◇◇◇◇◇

Follow my column in HEAS *and my private blog, the* Enchantasia Insider, *for all the latest happenings at Royal Academy post-curse!*

WE'VE GOT COMPANY

The good news is no matter how bad things are, we still have pie!"

Logan slides a tray of three steaming-hot apple pies with golden flaky crusts across the crammed table toward us. I can smell them from here. Where's my fork?

"That looks amazing," says Corden, licking his lips.

"Dig in." Logan wipes his hands on his chef jacket pockets as we all clamor for the one knife to cut the pies. Prue reaches it first. "There should be enough forks. Who was on cleaning duty last night? Prue?"

Prue looks up from cutting herself a slice. "Um…no, that was Heath."

Heath bats his long eyelashes. "No, I washed Tuesday

night. It was Devin's turn. Or maybe it was Sasha's. Was it my sister's?"

"Oh no, don't you put this on me!" Raina starts.

Everyone starts bickering.

Life post-curse (as everyone is referring to it) is a bit different, and not just because we're living in the Royal Underground. The entire mall area has been taken over by royals sleeping in tiny pop-up castles, on blow-up beds, and in sleeping bags. Most of us didn't run to Fairy Tale Reform School. (What? You think I'm going to trust Rose after what she pulled when we were outlaws? She tried to turn us over to Olivina! No thanks.) When the Battle of Rumpelstiltskin began, Headmaster Pierce led most of us down here instead, while my father lead a group of parents at the ball in the fight. I've heard rumors that the wicked stepmother's daughters, Azalea and Dahlia, took some RA kids with them to FTRS to engage in the fighting as well, but it's so packed down here I can't imagine it was a large group.

I'll admit, the first few days were frightening. Being underground, we didn't know what had happened to the rest of the kingdom. Pierce wouldn't let anyone out to see what was going on, so all I could do was wonder whether the school I had fought so hard to leave had been destroyed.

Were my parents alive? Was the royal court? I even began to wonder if all my ill will toward RA led to this, but I know that's crazy. Being underground that long can make you think strange thoughts. Thankfully, Lily made her way down to us and gave us updates on what was going on aboveground. The curse was stopped, the royal court was saved, but there was a lot of damage to the kingdom, and hearing that, Pierce made us continue to stay put till Snow gave the all clear.

Once the magic mirror system was up and running again, Snow got word to us that the kingdom was still standing, my parents were okay (and my dad was an asset in battle), but we needed to stay put for now. As to what our parents are going to do about us all going to school post-curse, I have no clue. I've heard some kids say we're all going to be sent home when it's safe. Others fear we're going to be stuck down here for months (please, no), while others think their parents are going to sign them out of here even if Royal Academy is up and running again in the near future.

As for us, we're still stuck underground listening to vanilla updates from Milo the Magic Mirror of the "We are a royal family, and royals can get through anything!" variety. My only real reports from the outside world are from Lily, who has been sneaking back out of the Underground to find food and keeps bringing small, injured animals to heal. The tales I've heard about the battle from the raccoons and possums are hairy and filled with explosions, red skies, and raging battles.

I feel guilty that we're down here doing nothing to help. We're spread out everywhere—from Marta's shop to Charmed, I'm Sure to the bookstore and near the fountains. Since we've been asked to stay in place for the time being, Logan, Corden, and several other students have joined with Charmed, I'm Sure and other eateries to start cooking for everyone.

I have to say, we all agree the food is really good.

Who's in charge of doing dishes is a different story.

Sasha drops a stack of forks on the table with a loud clang. "It was my turn. Here you go."

Everyone dives over the table to claim a fork.

"You know, I never thought I'd miss the pixies, but I do," says Logan as he shoves an oversize piece of apple pie in his mouth. "They might have been tricky, but they kept the cafeteria sparkling. There was never a lack of forks." He sighs.

"I'm sure we'll be back in the cafeteria in no time," Brynn says brightly. "Once the headmasters feel it's safe, they'll allow us to return to school, classes will resume, and the kingdom can go about the business of rebuilding." Her jaw is firm. "We will show the villains that evil never wins and help our kingdom thrive again."

"And how long do you think that will take?" Heath asks. "I'm kind of getting restless down here. Even the Charmiccinos have lost their appeal."

"Yesterday the unicorn I wished for only appeared for thirty seconds," Corden says dejectedly. "And they seem to have run out of marshmallow topping."

"And glitter sprinkles," Raina says, looking equally disappointed. "Plus, I'm growing tired of this dress, which I never thought I would." She looks down at the ball gown she's been wearing since last week. Thank the fairies there is a perfumery down here because we're all getting quite ripe.

"Are you guys really complaining about the lack of sprinkles and marshmallows?"

I turn to see a new fork hovering in the air over the pie. Tara.

She dives into the crowd of arms and pulls out a huge piece of cherry pie. This is the first time I've seen her in days.

"I'm with Brynn. We're lucky we're safe down here and

we have such luxuries as pies," Tara says, slipping the piece into her mouth. "You want me to tell you about the week in the Hollow Woods when Corden, Prue, and I lived off cricket and grasshopper soup?"

Lily flicks her tongue in support of this decision. Corden, however, looks almost green. "We swore we'd never talk about that again."

Tara laughs. An actual laugh. Maybe she's coming around. At first, we didn't even think she'd made it to the Underground. She hadn't attended the commendation ceremony and was nowhere to be found, but when we were shepherding kids down to the Underground, she was already here, telling people where to go. Being locked away down here, strangely enough, seems to have been good for her, much like the woods were once upon a time. It feels good to see her eating pie.

"I will keep my promise if you keep your promise to never again complain about a lack of marshmallows or sprinkles." Tara spears another forkful of pie. "What is a Charmiccino anyway?"

Everyone starts to explain at the same time before they are interrupted by the sound of bells and an alarm on Milo's mirrors.

"Greetings, students!" Milo addresses us pleasantly (in

part because Prue reprogrammed him to be less snarky). "We hope you are enjoying your breakfast. The weather outside today is sunny and cool, but in the Underground it's a delightful..."

Corden groans. "Here we go with another 'For your safety, you must stay down in the Underground another day' message!"

"I have an important announcement today. Your headmasters will be addressing all of you in the main Underground corridor in the next fifteen minutes. Please move in an orderly fashion to that area for further instructions."

Well, this is new. A cheer rises from somewhere down the hall.

"We're being sprung!" Heath says.

"Think they're starting school again?" Logan asks.

"Or sending us home?" Raina wonders.

"Let's not spread rumors." I scramble to stand up and can't help but be excited. Is this it? The moment everything changes, and I get to go home where I belong and focus on creature care? "Snow hasn't said anything to you?" I ask Heath.

"No, but Snow would never make us assemble just to say,

'Be patient,'" Heath explains as he rolls up his sleeping bag as if it's no longer of use. "She must be letting us out of here."

"Then what are we waiting for?" Sasha cries. "Let's go!"

We don't hesitate. Pie is forgotten, forks are dropped, and everyone immediately begins sidestepping over blow-up beds and around tiny pop-up castles to make their way to the large common area where the mall sometimes has flea markets with local vendors or the occasional concert during normal times. Instead, we find ourselves staring at the small stage that is now filled with adults, including the headmasters and some people I don't recognize. The woman to Snow's right is rather frightful with her salt-and-pepper hair whipped up into a tight bun. She's wearing a prim, plum-colored dress held closed at the collar with a glass slipper brooch.

Next to her is someone I recognize from *Happily Ever After Scrolls'* sketches—dark hair, raven on her shoulder, high black collar, and mahogany cape. Her bright-red lips are pulled into a thin line. Her coal-colored eyes take in the lot of us with a mixture of disinterest and what appears to be rage, and I know for certain it's the Evil Queen. They say she's reformed and helped take down Rumpelstiltskin (she's even made amends with Snow), but she's still an intimidating sight.

"Good morning, children," Snow addresses the crowd that is still gathering. "I apologize for keeping you down here so long, but your safety has been our top concern. You've been so patient while we sorted things out, and I'm grateful for how beautifully you've all behaved. Aside from that one late-night incident at Charmed, I'm Sure, you've all been splendid!"

(One night when we couldn't sleep, Heath decided to open up Charmed, I'm Sure and attempt to make Charmiccinos at 3:00 a.m. even though he'd never made one before. He wound up accidentally blowing up a prep table during the wish portion of the drink. Snow wasn't amused.)

"We've been in constant touch with your parents, many of whom joined the Battle of Rumpelstiltskin." At his name, one boy bursts into tears. "But that battle is over. You are safe. I'm fine. The royal court is fine. We are all fine," she says, acknowledging the others onstage with her. "And you are too. The fighting has ended. The villains have been vanquished, and Enchantasia is ours." She leads us all in awkward applause and looks to the others standing with her.

"I can't deny, however, that our kingdom has changed. This battle has opened our eyes to the villainy that darkened our doorsteps. We need to be vigilant going forward to keep it at bay. We need to trust in those we've never trusted before and work together. That's why I wanted to bring you together to introduce you to some new faces before we let you go upstairs." She smiles. "And yes, that means you get to leave the Underground today."

There is another round of cheers. I find even I'm getting excited about this conversation.

Headmaster Pierce steps forward. "When you step outside the Underground this morning, you will see a changed kingdom. While Royal Academy itself did not sustain much damage, there are bombed-out walls in our castle, the sound of construction hammering twenty-four seven inside and outside the castle, the village, and even at the royal court headquarters. Many have lost their homes, their schools, and their livelihood. It will take time for us all to rebuild, but we will, and we will be stronger because of it. Do not be frightened by any of this. We will get through this together and all pitch in to help during these trying times."

Brynn's hand shoots into the air. "How can we help, sir?"

"Thank you, Ms. Haun." Pierce smiles gratefully. "The best way any of you can help is to welcome the new students that will be joining our school in the interim. Classes will be resuming this coming week." There are a few groans.

My heart sinks. So school *is* back in session. But that doesn't mean all our parents will want us to stay here. I keep listening.

"We're a bit short-staffed with some still recovering from injuries sustained in battle, so classes will be combining in some areas, and we've had to appeal to teachers in other kingdoms to join us. But none of this is something you should worry about. What you need to focus on is school, and classes are resuming with some bonus students in them, which is quite exciting." He pauses. "Starting today, we will be sharing our school with the students of Fairy Tale Reform School."

"What?" someone cries. "No!" A few kids burst into tears.

Sasha and I look at each other. This I did not see coming. Immediately, there is an uproar.

"You want us to go to school with future villains?" another shouts.

Headmaster Pierce jumps in. "This is a temporary situation, but one that we feel benefits all the children of Enchantasia and is in keeping with the true royal spirit of our school—to help those in need. Fairy Tale Reform School was badly damaged in the Battle of Rumpelstiltskin, and they need somewhere to work and go to school during construction." There are continued murmurs throughout the crowd.

"We've spoken at length to Headmistress Flora of FTRS, and we both agree that keeping the children of this kingdom together and safe is extremely important," Snow continues. "We don't want any of you in harm's way when Olivina is still on the loose, which is why they'll be sharing our dorm space and classrooms."

"She can't be serious," Raina is mumbling next to me. "My sister has lost her mind. This is a terrible idea!"

Raina is right. There is no way my parents will stand for this. Mother is always complaining about the kids in the village who need a good sentencing to FTRS. She won't want her precious royal daughter going to school with them, however temporarily. While I think Mother can be a royal snob, being royal may work to my advantage here.

"Some of your classes will be here at RA, while others might be held in the one section of FTRS that is still standing," Headmaster Pierce adds. This only gets people crazier. "I know this is unprecedented, but I assure you we've given this a lot of thought."

"You want us to go to Fairy Tale Reform School?"

"It isn't safe! They're villains!"

"Why can't some other school take them?" someone asks.

"Some other school?" The Evil Queen's nostrils flare as she speaks up for the first time. Immediately people quiet. "Flora, are you hearing this?" She turns to the gray-haired woman next to her.

"I can answer that," Headmistress Flora says in a clipped tone. "Because of our long-standing connection to some of the royals at this school"—she clears her throat—"we appealed to RA first. It's the closest school to our own, distance-wise, and since we share much of the same curriculum for core classes, it made more sense than Jack of All Trades in the village."

"If FTRS is still standing, why can't they stay there?" someone yells.

"To answer that rather rude question…" the Evil Queen butts in. "The ELF Construction Company won't allow us to stay in the dorms. Something about curses, counterhexes, and the fact that we magically regrew parts of the school via golden egg without a permit." She rolls her eyes. "Not that we have to answer to the lot of you for our reasoning."

I may have hoped this would get me out of RA, but I

can't handle how our classmates are acting. "This is getting out of hand," I say to Heath. "We all sound so privileged and rude! Some people lost everything in this battle! These kids lost their school! Can you imagine what the Fairy Tale Reform School students would think if they could hear us?"

Heath grimaces. "I know. This is not painting royals in the best light."

"This is outrageous!" I hear Clarissa say, validating Heath's point. "Our parents won't go for this! This is not what they agreed to send us to Royal Academy for!"

"I can assure you, Ms. Hartwith, that your parents are well aware of our predicament," Snow says swiftly.

I pale. *All? No. Mother wouldn't agree to this.*

"We are all being asked to make sacrifices," Snow continues. "Right now, in order to serve *all* the children of this kingdom, we need to share our castle. Sharing is the royal way, as you know, and I believe under the circumstances, the more we put ourselves in our fellow citizens' shoes, the better we can grow to understand one another as a kingdom at large."

My heart is pounding. Snow can't mean my family. I was counting on them to put their foot down so I could go home and work with creatures. They want me to stay?

"But they're villains! You want us to become villains?" a voice shouts.

There is a crash and then a wave of voices echo through the Underground. I turn and see a sea of students in blue uniforms arriving in the Underground. They head straight toward the stage. They look as happy as we are to be here.

"These students are here to meet you and quite frankly, Snow and I are both appalled at your reactions," Pierce says, a distinct edge to his voice. "This is a temporary situation due to completely unforeseeable circumstances. Instead of focusing on the negative, we hope—no, *we expect*—our fine students to rise to the challenge. How do we expect to stop villainy if we can't get along with those whose backgrounds differ from our own?"

I agree with Pierce and can't help but feel ashamed for the lot of us, no matter how much I want to go home.

I feel a tap on my shoulder and turn around. It's Emerson.

"Oh good, Devin, I found you!" she coos. "As soon as Snow is done speaking, I'd love to get you and a few of your friends up on the stage with some of the Fairy Tale Reform School students arriving. We want to get a sketch for *Happily Ever After Scrolls*."

"What? Why?" Sasha and Raina gather around me.

Emerson smiles brightly. "If you're on board with schooling with villains, then your classmates will be too. The royal court wants all of you to be great school spokespeople during this merger."

"Oh, I don't think I'm staying at RA," I say, and my friends look at me. "I don't think my parents would agree to this."

Emerson winks. "Already talked to them." She grabs my arm. "Come on! Let's get you onstage!" She starts dragging me through the crowd, which seems to be getting ugly. My friends follow as people continue to shout.

"These kids are the ones responsible for the Battle of Rumpelstiltskin, and now you want us to go to school with them?" an RA kid yells and others chime in. "No way!"

"Hey! How do we know you brat royals aren't the whole reason Rumpelstiltskin attacked in the first place?" says someone from FTRS.

"Don't get lost," Emerson says, depositing me at the side of the stage with my friends. "I'll be back in a jiff!"

An RA kid with wavy brown hair turns to us. "Can you believe what they're proposing?"

"It's definitely unexpected," Sasha says, "but it could be enlightening, don't you think?"

"No way!" he says. "You heard about that Cobbler girl's sister, right?" We shake our heads. "I don't know her name. Hannah, I think. She teamed up with Rumpelstiltskin and practically ended us all. My mother's aunt's cousin's hairdresser's assistant said Hannah got sentenced to Fairy Tale Reform School after the Battle of Rumpelstiltskin." His eyes widen. "And now she'll be going here with us!"

"No. That can't be, can it?" Raina asks. She and Logan hold on to each other.

I look up at the teachers and former villains talking. Drooping dragons, that girl is definitely going here. And if they're willing to allow that, then what else are they changing to make all of this work? My heart starts to pound. *Please don't say you're getting rid of the remaining creature care classes. Please.*

"You royals need to grow a spine!" someone screams. There's a loud, raucous cheer from the back of the hall.

"Manners!" barks the Evil Queen.

Silence washes over the crowd as the students in blue take their places next to the RA kids on stage.

"Ah, yes, here they are! Children, please join me in welcoming the Fairy Tale Reform School students." Snow is trying to muster excitement, but even she looks slightly unnerved standing so close to the Evil Queen.

FTRS kids stand to the right of the teachers, and RA kids on the left—we all glare at one another.

"We are looking forward to you getting to know one another," Pierce tells all assembled, "and you will. With the extra number of students we will be housing, and double the class sizes, we have had to make adjustments to some of the elective classes. I'm sorry to say that a number will need to be pulled temporarily to accommodate so many new core classes."

"What? *No!*" I cry. That definitely includes creature care. I knew it! That's all I had going for me at this point. My blood begins to boil. First Snow says it's best if I stay here. Then she promises me new classes, and now she's taking them away? This has gone too far.

"Royal brats! Royal brats! Royal brats!" the FTRS kids start chanting.

"Villains! Villains! Villains!" Clarissa leads a counter cheer picked up by the RA students.

"Devin! Do something!" Emerson hisses from the side of the stage.

Me? Why me? Tara has disappeared. Logan is

hyperventilating. ("I've heard some of those FTRS kids have pet dragons! I can't live with someone with a pet dragon!") Sasha snaps her finger, and her magical quill immediately starts documenting what's happening. Heath and Raina look to the podium to guidance.

"You're losing them, Sis," Heath whispers to her on stage.

"Silence!" the Evil Queen booms and the room goes quiet. "We have much bigger problems than whether any of you like each other! The decision has already been made so go back to your rooms and make space for your new roommates to join you." No one moves. Her dark eyes flash. "*Go!*"

Frightened students on both sides of the aisle start to disperse, but I'm still here, staring at Snow. I have to say something about the creature care classes. She can't do this to me. If I'm staying put, I *need* these classes.

"Wait!" Emerson cries. "I wanted to get a sketch of the new FTRS students together with our heroes! Wait!" But Headmistress Flora and the Evil Queen have already moved on and are chatting quietly with Snow and Pierce about some new teacher they just hired named Princess Dragonfly.

"I don't know where we're supposed to fit another

roommate!" Raina complains. "My wardrobe closet barely holds all my frocks as it is. Devin, you could probably spare some room in yours since you don't like gowns. Devin? Devin, where are you going?"

Maybe I'm being impulsive, but this conversation with Snow can't wait. I approach the teachers at the same time a Fairy Tale Reform School student does from the other side of the stage.

"You can't do this!" we say at the same time and then look at each other.

The girl narrows her eyes at me. She has shoulder-length brown hair, big blue eyes, and a smattering of freckles across her nose. I notice she is wearing lace-up boots with her uniform. The other FTRS girls don't have boots on. Nor do they have ribbons in their hair.

"Headmistress Snow, please, reconsider dropping elective classes," I speak up, not letting the girl get in a word edgewise. "You can't take away our only creature care class. You promised you'd have one for me if I stayed!"

"Devin, I…" Snow starts, but her voice is drowned out by the girl who is yelling at the wicked stepmother.

"You can't make us live at RA! This is a bad move! I can feel it!" she complains. "Once these royals find out who I am, they will be out for blood. You're basically sending me to my death."

"Anna, please don't be so dramatic," the Evil Queen drawls. "I swear, you're just like your sister. You'll be fine."

Anna. Could Anna be the Hannah that boy was talking about?

"No, I won't," she says. "When they know who I am and what I've done, they'll be against me. You're setting me up to fail."

"Fail!" I say, taking the word and using it to my advantage. "That's what I'm going to do if I have no creature care classes. You promised me if I stuck around, I'd get what I need to hone my skills."

"Well, a lot has happened since our meeting, Devin," Snow says, sounding weary. "I can't help it if half the kingdom was under attack and I had to change the curriculum!"

"But..." I try.

"But..." I hear Anna say.

Then I hear someone laugh. "Oh, these two are quite the difficult ones, aren't they?"

We both turn around.

"Princess Rose," I say in surprise. She's wearing a teal

gown and has her blond hair piled up on her head in braids. "What are you doing here?"

"Helping run things, of course," Rose says cheerily. "We all have to pitch in during times like this."

"You?" I sputter. "You can't! You're…you're…a…"

"I think the word you're looking for is 'villain,'" Rose says calmly, and there is a gasp from everyone onstage. The Anna/Hannah girl snorts. "And no, I'm not. I was questionable for a time, yes, but I helped during the battle and redeemed myself." Her smile is thin. "And I know exactly how to handle your predicament, and Anna's here. Let's have them room together, shall we? They can duke it out and leave us out of it."

"Oh, that does sound fun," the Evil Queen says with a wicked smile.

"That actually might work," Headmistress Flora agrees and Snow nods her head.

"I'm not rooming with her!" we both say, outraged.

"She caused the Battle of Rumpelstiltskin!" I cry.

"She's a stuck-up royal brat!" Anna seethes.

Rose claps her hands excitedly. "It's decided then! Girls, meet your new roommate!"

NOT PART OF THE PLAN

N ice going, Devin," Raina grumbles as the two of us attempt to slide her bed across the room to make room for a few more beds. "Of all the Fairy Tale Reform School kids you could have had placed with us, it had to be the one that practically erased the kingdom!"

"I find it fascinating!" Sasha says as she clears off half her desk and bookcase to make space for the newcomers. "I don't know what the rest of the girls will be like, but think of the inside scoop I'll have on the big battle with Anna as our roommate." Her face takes on a determined look. "I just have to get her to trust me."

"I don't think that girl wants to be close with anyone!" I warn. "She called me a stuck-up royal brat. *Me!* I'm like the least royal person I know!"

"So true," Raina agrees, and I give her a look. "Sorry. I'm just thinking of your whole 'I don't want to rule; I just want to wear pants and talk to squirrels' thing."

"Regardless!" I say. "I'm telling you, this Anna is bad news. I wouldn't be surprised if she actually knew where Olivina was hiding!"

"No!" Sasha gasps and her quill flies off her desk, prepared to start taking a statement. "You think?"

"Not really," I add hastily. "I just meant because she was friends with Rumpelstiltskin and Alva."

The minute I stormed away from Snow and the teachers, I found my dove pal Demetris and had him give me the scoop on Anna's part in the Battle of Rumpelstiltskin. Apparently Anna turned on her sister, Gilly, and teamed up with the villains to try to enact the curse. In the end, she had a change of heart and helped her sister stop the curse. Sounds fishy if you ask me.

"Well, I guess if she sentenced herself to FTRS, she's trying to learn to be good so we should give her a chance," Raina decides.

I snort. "No thanks. We've already faced down villains and granddaughters of villains who are confused by their heritage. I don't want any more drama in my life." I just want to get through this transition with the FTRS kids and hopefully find a way to get myself out of here.

"Devin has a point," Sasha says. "What if Anna hates my blog or the fact my quill is always taking notes for me?"

"Or she needs more room in the wardrobe closet?" Raina worries. "I am not getting rid of any of my dresses."

"Or she's allergic to animals?" I wonder aloud. "Demetris has been bringing me sparrows and cardinals who need help, and who knows how many small creatures will be knocking on our door for aid now that they know we're back in the castle."

"Speaking of which, could you please ask the birds not to poop on my bedspread?" Raina says stiffly. "Without ladies-in-waiting anymore, the cleaning is up to me."

"Fair enough." I point to a small area of the room where I have a few supplies, which Lily hid in our room during the fighting. "I'll just use this space to work. No more poop."

"Thank you," Raina says.

There is a tinkling of bells, and the mirror in our room starts to swirl green, blue, and pink. "Good afternoon, students! Please have your rooms ready for your new roommates by four today. Also, please check your mini magical scrolls for your new class schedules."

The three of us dive over the beds to reach our scrolls and quickly tap them. "Yes!" Raina says at the same time Sasha and I yell "No!"

"Mine is exactly the same," Raina says with glee. "I still have Long May They Reign: A History of Royals in Power and all my other classes."

"Me too," Sasha says.

"Then why are you complaining?" I ask.

She turns her magical scroll to face me. "My Royals and the Media: Can't We All Just Get Along seminar is now being taught by Emerson Emet."

We all groan.

"What about your schedule, Devin? All good?" Raina asks cautiously, ready to swing my scroll away before I can break it in anger. She knows me so well.

I take a deep breath and look. History of Enchantasia, Breaking the Myth of the Glass Slipper, Fairy Tale Myths and Legends, Reigning 101… All the royal staples are there, but where are the creature care electives Snow promised? There's only one here, Care of Magical Creatures, and it's not held in the castle. It's at Fairy Tale Reform School!

I growl in frustration.

"Devin, why don't we head down to the Underground for a Charmiccino," Raina says soothingly. "Or something at Little Miss Muffin's?" She pulls the scroll from my hand.

"Raina, no one wants to go back to the Underground. We were there for weeks," Sasha says. "Give her space."

"I need to talk to my parents," I say aloud.

"That's a good idea!" Raina sounds perky. "I have some scented stationery right here and a quill with lavender ink. It gives letters such a nice touch. I don't think the Pegasus Post has come yet so your letter could go out this evening and—"

"No." My voice doesn't sound like my own. I stare pointedly at Sasha. "I need to talk to my parents today."

"That's impossible unless you're going to take a Pegasus to your house," Raina says with a laugh.

Sasha and I look at each other.

"I'm not supposed to," she mumbles.

"You owe me," I remind her. "Need I remind you about the time I had Lily spy on that meeting between Storybook Palette and your sister and report back for your exposé on the ingredients in Beauty and the Blush?"

"I remember." Sasha sighs. "Close your eyes. Both of you."

"Me?" Raina complains. "I don't even know what you're both talking about!"

I close my eyes, hear some drawers slamming, and then feel a piece of cool metal pressed into my hand. I open my eyes and look down at the small gold item.

"Don't let anyone see you use that," Sasha warns. "And bring it right back when you're done."

"A compact?" Raina asks. "Why does Devin need powder?" She gives me a critical glance. "You do look a tad shiny, but it's just your nose."

"I will bring it right back! Thanks!" I head to the door without explaining.

"No one can find out I have that," Sasha adds hurriedly. "It's still in the testing stages! It may glitch!"

I don't care. I clutch the compact tightly and race out of our dorm room. The halls are packed with girls rearranging rooms and tossing out things to make space for new beds. Pixies fly through the halls making people crazy ("You have six new roommates!" one giggles), while griping can be heard from various rooms about the new sleeping arrangements. "Where do they expect me to keep six dozen gowns if I have to make room for more beds?" I hear Clarissa sob. Ball gowns, crystal balls, and giant makeup cases all litter the floor as I jump over items in my quest to get down the winding staircase. I reach a fancy wooden door at the bottom of the stairs that leads outside and grab the handle.

"Sorry! That door is closed off for construction," says an elf in a construction helmet. "You need to go down three doors to the right and make a left turn, then go down that hall and take the second door on the left side. But if that's blocked off too, you..."

"You've got to be kidding me." I race off, not listening to the rest of his speech. I find a door that isn't covered with caution tape or nailed over, so this must be the door he was talking about. I turn the knob.

"I'm sorry, but where do you think you're going?"

I spin around. The only person in the corridor is me, but there's a mirror flashing orange. "Milo?"

"No, this is Miri," says a clipped female voice. "And I cannot allow you to go out that door."

"Miri? I don't know a Miri." I turn the knob and open it.

"*Stop!* I'm from Fairy Tale Reform School, and I just received privileges at Royal Academy since we're sharing quarters for the time being. My job is to keep students in line. I was told no one could go outside without permission."

Leaping lizards, she's got to be kidding me. Maybe I can butter her up. "Miri, did you say? I love that we're getting a new mirror around here who can keep things in order. You have no idea what can go wrong in a castle this size."

"Oh, I can imagine," she says. "Our place is pretty large too."

"Now that you say your name, I realize I have heard of you," I say cheerfully. "I've heard you're aces at your job!"

"You have? I mean—I am!" Miri says, sounding brighter.

"Between us, way better than Milo," I whisper. "At least, that's what I heard Snow say."

"Well, I don't want to speak for Snow, but I am very good," Miri agrees.

"So listen, Miri, I just need to go out this door for five minutes." She starts to protest. "I can promise I'm going no farther than a few feet and since you haven't officially been announced to the students yet as having privileges here, maybe you can make an exception?"

"Maybe," Miri says slowly.

"I can even leave this door open so you can hear me talking. And I'll come right back in and tell everyone I know how amazing Miri is compared to Milo, who can't hold a candle to you. We've never had a mirror swirl with such vibrant orange colors."

Miri's mirror turns bright pink. "I pride myself on my color wheel. It's the most elaborate of all mirrors at showing emotion."

"I can tell," I say solemnly. I want to use the compact so badly that it's practically burning a hole in my hand. "So do we have a deal?"

She sighs. "Deal. But five minutes! Otherwise I sound the alarm."

"Thank you!" I slip out the door. This is my first time on the grounds, and for a second, I am too stunned to move. Part of a castle wall is charred, and there are some downed trees and something still smoking in the distance. Elves are fixing a window on the other side of the castle, and a crane is being used to fix the ballroom roof. Hearing about the damage and seeing it for myself are wildly different. No wonder they kept us in the Underground for so long! But if things are on the mend, maybe my parents will see reason. I take a deep breath, open the compact, rub my finger on the glass in a circular motion like I saw Sasha do the time I caught her using this, and say who I want to contact.

"The Nile residence of Cobblestone Creek, please."

I watch the mirror swirl like the ones in the castle, and then a bright-yellow light glows from the glass and explodes like glitter. Suddenly my parents are staring back at me.

"Devin?" Mother asks, peering so close her nose is against the glass. "Is that you? My word. What are you doing in our mirror?"

Fairy be! It worked!

"Hi, Mother!" I say excitedly. "Is Father there too?"

"Yes, I'll get him. But I still don't understand. How are you doing this?"

"Magic." I couldn't explain this if I tried. One day I caught Sasha using what she called a prototype of correspondence that would put the Pegasus Post out of business. Only the royal court had access to the gadgets, but Sasha stole Rose's and now we have it even if we're not supposed to use it. Desperate times call for desperate measures. "Look, I don't have much time. I need to speak to you both."

"Devin?" Father appears in the mirror. Dark lines rim his eyes and he's got three-day-old stubble. He's been working nonstop, I'm sure.

"Father! It's good to see you."

"What are you doing with a gabber?"

Is that what it's called? "I, uh…"

"What's a gabber?" Mother asks.

"No one has those but the royal guard and the royal court." Father's voice sounds like a warning. "Devin, how did you…"

"How is not important," I interrupt. "What is important is how badly I need to get out of Royal Academy. It's not safe here anymore. They're housing the Fairy Tale Reform School students at our school!"

"What?" Mother is aghast. "That can't be. We haven't heard anything about that."

"I have," Father says, afraid to look at her. "Emerson Emet told me all about it, and I said it's fine. The situation is temporary. They'll be together a few months at most."

"A few months?" Mother cries.

I can tell Mother is upset, so she's the one I need to appeal to. I lay it on thick. "We have to bunk with them, Mother, and all our classes are being combined. Some of mine are even at what's left of Fairy Tale Reform School! I only have one creature care class now. From Dragons to Yeti: How to Care for Creatures Who Want to Eat You—the one

I was most looking forward to because we got to work with dragons—is on hold! And now Emerson wants me to be a role model to the FTRS kids and bond with Anna Cobbler, who is my new roommate. You know, the girl who helped Rumpelstiltskin with his curse?"

Mother gasps. "You can't dorm with a criminal! She's a villain in training!"

I knew Mother would see it my way.

"I have no choice," I say sadly. "All the other rooms are full. But there is an alternative."

"Yes?" Mother says eagerly.

"Let me leave Royal Academy." I hold the compact closer to my face so they can see me clearly. "I'm not happy here. I haven't been since day one. We all know what I want to do—creature care—and I could do that at Nottingham, far away from villains or kids from Fairy Tale Reform School. Isn't that a better alternative? Doing something I love where I could get real training?" I stare at my parents.

"Skies are falling, curses are being cast, and beanstalks are shooting out of the sky," I add. "Our kingdom is changing, and I think it is time I change with it. Let me use my gift—the same gift Olivina sought me out for—and train and then come back and help my kingdom the best way I know how. By being a magical creature caretaker." I wait to hear their response. They're so quiet I can hear hammering behind me and someone named Earl telling Mark he's headed on his lunch break. Mother whispers something to Father and I wonder. Could my passionate speech have swayed her? She's gesturing with her hands, but I can't hear what she's saying.

I feel a small tug at the bottom of my dress and look down. It's a family of mice.

Are you the creature caretaker? one squeaks. *Timmy has been limping since the battle, and we were hoping you could look at his back right paw.*

I squeak in response. *No problem! Just give me a minute here.*

"Devin? Are you squeaking?" Mother narrows her eyes at me. "What's going on?"

"So what do you say?" I press, not wanting to get sidetracked. "Can I apply to Nottingham? Come home? I don't fit in here."

Mother looks at Father. My hope swells.

"No," Father says.

My jaw drops. "But, Father—"

"Devin, I'm sorry. It's just not safe for you to be anywhere but Enchantasia right now."

"It's not safe *in* Enchantasia!" I argue. Even my mother looks surprised at his decision.

"It's safer here than Nottingham or anywhere else," he says. "I'm sorry, but with Olivina on the loose, we cannot let our guard down. The protection at Royal Academy, aided by the former villains who teach at Fairy Tale Reform School, can't be topped. You will be safe there, and your safety is our top concern right now."

"But…" The mouse family is looking up at me as one of my hot tears falls from my face and hits the baby mouse on the head.

"Darling, we do hear you, but think of it this way… You're getting a top education at Royal Academy," Mother says. "You'll emerge well rounded, and then if you want to help the little furry critters while you're attending to your royal duties, I'm sure you can do that too. But for now, I think your father is right. You need to stay right where you are. You're safe. That's what matters. Devin, you didn't see what we saw that night of the Battle of Rumpelstiltskin." My mother's eyes widen and now she's crying. "I thought we were all done for."

"Till Olivina is captured, we need you to stay at Royal Academy," Father reiterates. "I'm sorry, Devin."

I look down at the mice sadly. I know how to fix and set a sprained paw but think of what I could do if I knew the correct herbs and ingredients to create pain relievers and antibiotics. For now, I'll have to settle for what I have.

Wait a minute...

"Father? You said *till* Olivina is captured. That means when she is captured and villainy is abolished, I can leave Royal Academy, right?"

"No one has been able to find her," Father says.

"But you might! You're hunting her now. A lot of people are. If you find her and it puts an end to villainy, can I apply to Nottingham?"

"And I would think you of all people, would embrace the FTRS kids coming to RA. You're all about including everyone and hating any kind of hierarchy."

Drooping dragons. Mother knows me better than I thought she did. "Well, yes, that's true," I squeak.

"So you're just pretending to be afraid so I'll worry too and bring you home?" Mother smirks triumphantly when I say nothing. "I thought so! You clever girl! Well, I'm not falling for it. If father feels you're safer there, then that's where you stay."

"Mother," I grumble. "I can take care of myself. I don't need protection!"

She sighs. "Oh Devin… Why are you pushing this? Don't you want to settle down with a cute prince like Heathcliff White and help rule a monarchy?"

I don't answer. I shouldn't have to. I've made my wants pretty clear. I've never cared about finding a prince. "Father? Do we have a deal?"

Father looks at Mother. "Yes. If we find Olivina and rid the kingdom of this final villain, we can talk about Nottingham."

"Thank you!" I gush. "Got to go. Love you! Bye!" I shut the compact before they can change their mind. I place it in my pocket and lean down to scoop up the mice family and bring them back to my dorm room.

You look happy, one squeaks.

I am, I squeak back.

That's because I'm not going to wait for Father to find Olivina. I'm going to do it myself.

HI, ROOMIE

From our dorm room window, I can see the line of students in bright-blue uniforms marching up one of the paths toward Royal Academy with their sacks and pillows. Raina, Sasha, and I are crammed around the window, watching them approach.

"I hear their hallways move and seal up on a regular basis to keep them from escaping," Raina says. "What's going to keep any of them from escaping from here?"

"I really hope I get some of their teachers as subs," says Sasha, looking excited. "The Big Bad Wolf is a teacher there and so is the Sea Siren. I want to take class in a room with a giant fish tank."

Lily flicks her tongue at Sasha. *Not polite.*

"Lily says you're being rude," I tell her. "You're not supposed to call a mermaid pool a fish tank."

Sasha blushes. "Sorry. I should know better."

"I don't think we're getting mer-students anyway," I say. "We don't have the accommodations for them. Lily heard the Sea Siren is teaching all the mer-kids at her lair in the ocean while Blackbeard the Pirate is taking several of the kids on an interactive voyage where they can learn how to be proper pirates."

"Who would want to be a proper pirate?" Raina asks.

"I would!" Prue says as she walks in with Brynn and Tara, who are holding pillows and bags. We rush over to help them.

"Are you guys our other new roommates?" I say excitedly.

"Yep!" Prue drops a large bag with a thud and the floor shakes. "Snow thought it was a good idea to let us all stick together. She said, 'If they can navigate the Hollow Woods, they can share one room.'"

I grin. This is the best news I've had since…I don't know when. It's just nice to have some good news after my conversation on the gabber, which Sasha promptly made me return and hid in a new location. Grimm forbid Rose learns she has it.

Rose. Can't believe she's here now too and made Anna our roommate!

But…deep breaths. I will find Olivina. And in the meantime, I have all of my friends in one room.

"So what's this about being a pirate?" Prue asks as she starts to set up her Royal Academy Security 3000 equipment on an empty desk. "I'd love some training."

"It's a curriculum some of the Fairy Tale Reform School kids have," I explain. "Too bad we don't have the option of spending a semester in the Hollow Woods."

Everyone groans.

"No thank you," Raina says. "I quite like having running water again."

"I think this new situation is going to be fun," Brynn says, hanging her bag on the back of the bed nearest to me. "We are going to get new perspectives on our kingdom. What do the Fairy Tale Reform School kids know that we at Royal Academy don't? How can we learn from each other?" She pulls a few scrolls out of her bag. "I already have a list of questions for our new roommate about FTRS and what life is like in the village. I've never lived there so I'm dying to learn all I can about it."

That's so Brynn. If anyone here is going to eventually be crowned, I have a feeling it's her.

There's a loud snort and we turn around. Tara has collapsed on Raina's bed, of all places, and fallen asleep.

"Um, Tara?" Raina taps her lightly. "Tara? This bed is mine." She laughs nervously. "See all the silk sheets and the aromatherapy pillow and sleep mask, not to mention the lavender-scented canopy? It's mine." She pokes Tara harder and the girl sits up.

"What?" Tara rubs her eyes. I notice they are rimmed with dark circles.

"Are you okay?" I ask.

"Just tired," Tara says, looking away. "I'm not sleeping well. I wake up more tired than rested."

"You're stressed," Prue says and looks at us. "Tara has finally agreed to take classes here, but some of our classmates have not been so welcoming."

I can't say I'm surprised. If students are giving her a hard time, she'll never start to settle in and want to stay. "Just tell us who it is. I'll send Lily into their room at night and tell her to bring her snake besties to scare them."

Lily flicks her tongue. *With pleasure!*

Tara smiles. "Thanks, but I'm sure the talk will die down, especially with the FTRS kids here now. So which bed is mine?" We point to an empty one that hasn't been made up yet. Tara crashes down on it and turns toward the wall.

"You're going to sleep great in here!" Raina says cheerily. "I'll spray lavender around the room before bedtime, and I have several extra sleep masks if you need one. Princess Rule 68: A well-rested royal is a productive royal."

"I thought you took her copy of the book away from her," I say to Sasha.

Sasha shrugs. "She keeps finding new ones."

"We've had a lot of changes the last few weeks," Prue admits. "I miss the sound of crickets and sleeping under the stars."

Lily flicks her tongue. *I love crickets!*

Tara sits up. "Me too. It's like I fall asleep and then I wake up an hour later and I can't fall back off, but then I do and I'm up again. I'm just restless, I guess."

She's also sleepwalking, Lily tells me. *I found her in the pumpkin patch last night.*

"Any chance you're a sleepwalker?" I ask gingerly. "That will make you super tired! Lily thought she saw you in the pumpkin patch last night."

"No." Tara's whole body stiffens. "Lily must have me mistaken for someone else. I don't sleepwalk." She glares at Lily. "You know, I don't need rumors spread about me again. I—"

"I'm sure she's wrong," I say.

I'm not, Lily hisses.

I know, I hiss back. *But I don't want to rock the boat.* For once, I'm thankful no one in this room speaks bearded dragon.

"Why rock the boat when you've got me to do it for you?"

Anna Cobbler throws her bag down on the last bed and looks at us defiantly, almost daring one of us to say something that will get us clobbered.

"Wait, do you speak bearded dragon?" I ask, surprised.

Anna rolls her eyes. "No. What makes you think that?" She begins pulling a few things out of her bag, including several bottles of Rapunzel's famed shampoo, a dragon-tooth hair comb, and a wooden brush. Her hair is clearly one of her favorite things. It's long, brown, and hangs to the middle of her back. She's tied it back with a blue polka-dot bow that pulls it into a ponytail.

Tara immediately stands up. "What are you doing here?"

Anna blinks. "Uh…moving in?"

"I saw you," Tara says. "Last night."

Anna attempts to skirt around her. "I don't know what you're talking about."

However, Tara follows. "Outside the castle. Near the vegetable garden. At school."

"You have me mistaken with someone else," Anna snaps. "I wasn't outside school last night."

"And neither were you," I say to Tara lightly. "Didn't you say you don't sleepwalk?" What's going on here?

"Sorry." Tara shakes her head and goes back to her bed, turning toward the wall again. "You're right. I'm just confused." She snatches one of Raina's sleep masks off the table behind her bed and puts the mask over her eyes. "If you guys don't mind, I'm just going to take a nap." The room is eerily quiet.

"*Awkward*," Sasha mouths to me.

"Hi. I'm Brynn!" Brynn rushes over to Anna to cut the tension, and Anna just looks at her.

"I'm new here too, as are Prue and Tara, although the two of them were here for a blip before Olivina banished them." She's talking fast. "Then she banished Devin, Raina, Sasha, and our other friends too, but they cleared their names with my help and now we're all here, so in a way, we're all starting fresh together." Brynn smiles. "We're really happy to have you here."

Anna smiles thinly. "Well, then that makes one of you." She looks around. "Maybe we should just get this out of the way now. If Devin Nile hasn't filled you in already, yes, I'm Anna Cobbler. Yes, I was part of the Stiltskin Squad. Yes, I went of my own free will." Something flickers across her face. "But in the end, I did what's right. I went against him and Alva. I helped my sister defeat him and ended the battle. *I asked* to be sentenced to Fairy Tale Reform School to change my wicked ways. So I don't need any of you reminding me how evil I once was."

"People make mistakes," Brynn says diplomatically. Anna's mouth twitches.

"How do you know my name?" I ask Anna suspiciously.

Anna looks me up and down. "You're not the only one who knows how to dig."

"Anna!"

A goblin girl wearing a string of pearls and dangly earrings appears in our doorway and throws a string-tied package of papers at her. "Here! You left these at FTRS."

"Oh. Sorry, Tessa." Anna clutches the parchment to her chest.

"Maybe you could stop disappearing and remember your own stuff for a change!" The girl slams the door behind her.

Sasha sidles up next to Anna. "Do you write too? Because I have my own blog and I'd love to interview—"

"*No.*" Anna plops down on the unmade bed, unties the papers, and starts sorting through them.

Brynn sits down on the bed next to her. "Are those letters?"

Anna sighs. "Look, I'm not here to make friends." She sees Brynn's expression and her own softens slightly. "I'm sure you're all perfectly nice, but I'm at FTRS to learn how to be…someone else. So whether I'm at that castle or this one, it doesn't matter. I just want to be left alone."

"Oh-*kayyy.*" Raina turns away to roll her eyes at me.

I nod in agreement, but strangely I kind of get it. This girl has a plan. Distractions—like friendships—will just bog her down. Maybe I should have done the same when I arrived. Then I wouldn't have gotten caught up in the whole Olivina mess. Then again, I wouldn't have gotten to know my roommates or Brynn, who are the bright spots of attending a school that has classes like Prim and Proper: How to Dress for Success as a Modern Royal.

"Greetings, Fairy Tale Reform School and Royal Academy students!"

The mirror in our room swirls cotton-candy pink and grassy-green.

"Hi, I'm Miri," comes a chipper voice.

"And I'm Milo," says a deeper voice.

"And together...we're your mirrors!" they say in unison.

"If we can get along and share our mirror time, then you can too," says Miri.

"And to prove it to all of you," adds Milo, "all Royal Academy and Fairy Tale Reform School students are invited to attend your first getting-to-know-you mixer tomorrow afternoon entitled 'Charmed to Meet You!'"

If I'm not mistaken, I hear the entire castle groan. Tara continues to snore.

"I'm not going," I declare.

"Neither am I," Anna seconds.

"Oh, and children? When Milo says 'invited,' he really means 'must attend.'" Miri's voice is tight. "There is no option here."

"We will also be sending around a poll via mini magical scroll this afternoon on various designs for a unity sash to be worn by all students during our time together," Milo explains.

"Though your uniforms—or dress choices—can remain the same while the schools are united, your headmasters thought it would be nice to have a symbol that unifies you as students."

"But we just got a new sash." Raina waves the Royal Is a State of Mind sash we got at our commendation-ceremony-that-wasn't.

"Not everyone here is royal," Anna reminds her. "Nor would we want to be."

"You know, your sister Gilly used to think like that too, but clearly she changed her mind," Sasha says.

"Yeah, well, I'm not Gilly and I never will be." Anna clutches her Pegasus Posts to her chest, lies down on the still unmade bed, and closes her eyes.

Happily Ever After Scrolls

Brought to You by FairyWeb—Enchantasia's
Number One News Source

The Hunt for Olivina

by Sasha Briarwood

Greetings, royal lovers! I'm Sasha Briarwood, here to reflect on the changes that have come to Royal Academy this past week. I can sum them up in one way: we've been taken over.

Yes, as you might have heard, due to the aftermath of the Battle of Rumpelstiltskin, Royal Academy and Fairy Tale Reform School have had to combine castles for the time being. We're sharing dorms, sharing cafeterias, sharing classes. We're even sharing teachers.

Who would have thought the sister of Sleeping Beauty would be learning Potions 101 from the Evil Queen? Not me! But for the love of Grimm, is it a nail-biter! I've been longing for some excitement in my life (that doesn't involve the kingdom being erased), and this is it.

So how long are we going to be living together? I went to the headmasters for answers and got this:

"When the time is right for the Fairy Tale Reform School students to return to their school, they will," Headmistress Snow said diplomatically.

On the other hand, Headmistress Flora of Fairy Tale Reform School said: "That's for the adults to know and the students to learn when it's time!"

Touchy.

As you can see, it's not going to be as quick as a sleepover. My sources are hearing this could go on for months. Or, at the very least, until Olivina is captured. She is the main villain on the loose now that Rumpelstiltskin and Alva have been vanquished, and the royal army won't rest till she's captured. My sources say they fear Olivina will not go quietly, and they wouldn't put it past her to try to get FTRS students to join her ranks and help her take over.

"There's no telling what she's capable of," said my source. "What if she chooses to enact the curse again herself? Or bring back Rumpelstiltskin and Alva? Or tries to invade

Royal Academy and take the students captive or brainwash them? We can't rest till we know Enchantasia is safe, and for that to happen, all students must be kept under watch together."

I hear the royal army is making some progress. This morning, they rounded up a large group of gargoyles found hiding in the Hollow Woods. "These gargoyles will be tried for their crimes in helping Alva and Rumpelstiltskin," said a royal guard spokesperson. "We won't rest till the remaining gargoyles are captured and questioned about Olivina's whereabouts."

Stay tuned for updates!

CHAPTER

8

GETTING TO (NOT) KNOW YOU

R ise and shine, students!" Miri the Magic Mirror says
cheerfully. "It's Charmed to Meet You Day!"

"Who will you be paired with for beanstalk climbing,
finding the magic lamp, or magic carpet races?" Milo chimes
in. "Your new bestie could be right down the hall or sleeping
in your dorm room already."

From across our crowded room Anna and I glare at each
other. No. Way.

"You never know till you get to know each other! So
come on out and meet on the grounds. The area has been
cleared for use by the royal guard, who did a thorough check
of the surrounding area. As did the Evil Queen, who placed

a protection charm over the whole area. So relax and have some fun!" Milo's mirror flashes a multitude of colors like fireworks. Then the glass fades to a dreary gray. "Attendance is mandatory!"

I glance at Tara's bed. She's snoring away. Anna has already left the room. Prue is combing her hair, while Sasha is the one who springs out of bed and heads behind the dressing partition first. When she emerges, she's dressed in pants and tall riding boots perfect for a day of running around in the mud after last night's rain. Lily was thrilled about the weather. Post-rain is the best time for her to catch insects so I suspect I won't see her all morning.

"Come on!" Sasha says. "Let's be the first ones there so we get to pick our own teams."

No one moves.

Even Lily is already up and out today. Post-rain is the best time for her to catch insects so I suspect I won't see her all morning.

Sasha sighs. "At least we get to do this instead of regular coursework today, right?" No one answers. Raina hasn't even removed her fluffy, pink sleep mask yet. "Guys, it's not going to be that bad! It will be fun!"

"This is miserable," Sasha grumbles. We are currently in the middle of a muddy field listening to the RA band play off-key while the Royal Academy kids glare at the Fairy Tale Reform School kids standing on the other side of the large field.

"I thought you said it would be fun?" I tease her.

In between the two groups, several activities have been set up. A corn maze is being timed by a rabbit with an oversize clock who keeps yelling, "You're late!" Two identical beanstalks are side by side, waiting to be climbed as part of a racing challenge, while a bobbing-for-poison-apples stand (kidding on the poison part) is off to the side. No one has approached it yet and I don't blame them. It's kind of creepy. A station with a wooden sign that says ON YOUR MARK features several archery targets of scarecrows that I think are supposed to resemble Olivina, Alva, and Rumpelstiltskin. In the distance, I see two gnomes doing test runs on a makeshift magic carpet racecourse. There's also a Pegasus petting zoo, which I find a bit distasteful, but I guess they have to do something with the Pegasi since they're grounded from doing riding lessons till Olivina is caught.

But no one is trying anything because all anyone is doing is staring at one another while Snow and Rose and some of the other teachers try to cheerlead us into participating.

"Look at that beanstalk! Isn't it beautiful!" Snow says as she walks by our side of the field. "Professor Harlow grew it herself this morning with a spell."

I pretend not to hear her, but I'm listening to the teachers' conversation like a hawk (who taught me all I know about concentration).

Professor Harlow trails behind, her long, purple cape billowing in the wind. "Even though I said repeatedly it was probably a bad move, considering Rumpelstiltskin used beanstalks to try to attack the kingdom!" She looks directly at me and scowls. "One of you better get out in the middle of this field, so help me before I…before I…"

"Harlow…temper," Headmistress Flora says as she tugs at the sash she's wearing over her dress. The sash flashes pink, then teal blue, then yellow while the words BETTER TOGETHER—RA AND FTRS! sparkle and glow. "These things are too tight! Rose? I'm not sure the uncomfortable sash is the way to go. Don't we have enough conforming going on here already?"

Rose frowns and looks at the scroll in her hands again. "Yes, but pins could be used to prick people, and the students voted down a hair bow or bow tie because they hate them, and a uniform seems silly when we aren't going to be together forever. Are we?"

"Not if I can help it," Harlow murmurs. "Speaking of help, where is the new staff? Aren't they starting today?"

"We don't call them staff, Harlow," Headmistress Flora sounds weary. "They're teachers, and Princess Dragonfly is right over there manning the poison-apple station."

I turn to see a tall, wiry woman with brown hair piled high on her head (giving her another two inches). She's standing by the apple buckets across the field. Clarissa is standing beside her chatting with a girl whose back is to us. I do a double take. Is that Tara? Is Clarissa introducing her to our new teacher? I see Tara awkwardly hold out her hand and shake the princess's. Then she hurries off. Clarissa stays by Princess Dragonfly's side, talking her ear off.

"Girls, please get out there," Snow begs us. "Maybe if you lead the charge, the others will follow."

Raina looks apprehensively from the beanstalk to the corn maze. "I'm not overly fond of activities that make me sweat."

"Same!" Logan says, running up and sounding out of breath already. "I also don't like anything with actual beasts or dragons, of course. Perhaps there is a Tom Thumb–wrestling challenge I could do?" he says brightly. "As long as you don't pair me with anyone who has a strangely large thumb that could break my thumb as I'm quite partial to having my thumbs, with all the time I spend in the kitchen."

"Forget Tom Thumb–wrestling!" says Heath, walking up behind him and putting an arm around his sister and Logan. "Let's try magic carpet racing. Being in the air will be nice, even if there is a flying height restriction." He looks at his sister.

"It's for your own safety," Snow reminds them. "That's why we grounded Pegasi for lessons too. Just for now. So get out there, please. For your favorite sister?" Raina glares at her. "Your favorite *older* sister?"

"But who am I going to race?" Heath grins. "Devin here?"

"You'd lose," I deadpan. "I am an excellent flyer."

Heath raises his right eyebrow. "Are you?"

"Yep," I say confidently. "I've learned from all the best birds and hawks. The key is all in how you manage wind speed."

"Prove it!" he says with a glint in his eye.

"You can't race Devin," Rose snaps. "She's from your own school. You need to pick an FTRS kid."

"None of them will challenge us." I motion to the group several yards away, standing with their arms folded defiantly. "Even our FTRS roommate left before us this morning and hasn't been seen since."

"I thought I saw Tara talking to that Clarissa girl," Prue says, "but now she's gone."

"There is no way Tara was talking to Clarissa," Raina says and Prue shrugs.

"Well, someone has to start the games, or we're just going to be standing here all day!" Rose starts to shove us forward. "Go on! Pick someone! Make us proud!" Rose cups her hands around her mouth and shouts, "GAMES ARE STARTING!" Then she tosses sashes at each of us and nudges us harder.

"Oww!" Sasha complains. "Stop pushing me!"

From the sidelines, I see something zoom by us in a flash, leaving sparkles in its wake. Suddenly there is a *POP* and the figure grows to full size. It's Emerson.

"Oh good! You're here and ready to play. And look how nice those sashes look!" Emerson says. "Get them on now. Go on." We place them over our heads. "Lovely! Now let's talk about who we can photograph you with for *HEAS*. As a show of unity. Devin? Maybe you could say a few words as well. I also need you to start organizing that mini magical scroll course on creature care you said you'd do."

"I..." I stumble, looking around for Brynn or Sasha, who are always ready to give speeches. I was hoping Emerson would forget about that scroll course as well. I need teaching. I'm not a teacher myself. "I don't even know what I'd say. We haven't played yet."

Squawk! Squawk!

Two geese fly overhead. *Storm brewing, Devin! Be careful out there today if you take to the sky!*

I squawk back *Thanks!* But truthfully there isn't a cloud in the sky.

"I'm sure you can think of something!" Emerson says impatiently. "What challenge do you want to try first?"

"Archery?" I guess. Seems harmless enough.

"Fine!" She leads me over to the FTRS kids, who all stare stonily at me. "Pick one to challenge."

I falter, looking at their angry faces. Trolls that look like I just announced they were being sent to the dungeons. Girls and boys who roll their eyes at the sight of my riding boots and pants. ("Of course they don't need to wear a uniform," one hisses.) And ogres that could probably break my arrow in one hand.

"Um…" I look down the line, hoping to spot Anna, but I don't see her. Instead, I focus on the green goblin girl who was yelling at Anna yesterday. Today she's wearing bright-pink earrings that match her pink dress and an even pinker sash that says ROYAL LADIES-IN-WAITING. Drooping dragons, what is that? At least she seems excited I am walking her way. "How about her?"

"*Yesss!*" she cries, fist-pumping the air. She runs over and starts shaking my hand vigorously up and down. "Hi! My name is Tessa Underlin. I'm the unofficial leader of the Royal Ladies-in-Waiting, and I think it's amazing that we're all here together under one roof."

"Splendid!" Emerson claps her hands excitedly and her quill takes notes next to her. "A willing participant. I told you this would work to our advantage. The rest of you go pick challengers while I help Devin here." She shoos my friends away.

Tessa can't stop talking. "You have no idea how hard it is to help royals when you're not anywhere near their castle to see their wants and needs! You know?" I open my mouth to respond but she keeps going. "So? Who are you related to? Snow? Rose? Rapunzel? Who? Please say you're related to Heathcliff White. He's the dreamiest prince here. You don't look familiar though." She steps back appraisingly. "You're not one of those new not-actually-royal-but-get-to-go-to-RA types, are you?"

"I'm royal, but I'm nobody...famous." I hold out my hand. "Devin Nile, future magical creature caretaker."

She stares at my hand. "But you're royal? And you want to hold a regular *job*?"

I can see we aren't going to see eye to eye on this issue. I look at Emerson. "Can we get the interview done, please?"

Twenty minutes later, Tessa and I have shot four rounds of arrows at targets, which has encouraged a few more groups of kids to team up for some tournament games. Once Tessa and I paired off, Heath introduced himself to a troll boy from FTRS, Logan met a fairy that is as allergic to dragons as he is, and Raina and Sasha both found kids willing to venture onto the beanstalks, which look rather cool, especially when I see all the birds hanging out on various stalks, chirping about a big storm. I'd love to get closer and talk to them, but Tessa is still busy giving Emerson her quotes for *HEAS*.

"Thank you for all that information, Tessa," Emerson says and looks back at me. "And now if you'd both just stand for a quick sketch."

"We're missing the other activities," I say, watching as Heath and his partner from FTRS go from the corn maze to the poison-apple bobbing station together. "And there are so many other groups you could be interviewing."

"I'd love a sketch." Tessa contradicts me, sidling up and looping her arm through mine. "It's not often a Royal Lady-in-Waiting makes *Happily Ever After Scrolls*!"

I sigh and stand still, looking around as the groups slowly merge. Students are not fighting or sticking to their own side of the lawn anymore. Headmasters Snow, Pierce, and Flora are walking around observing everyone and looking rather pleased…or annoyed whenever Princess Rose comes running by with the megaphone she's using to give a big speech.

"For too long this kingdom has suffered due to a great divide," she says. "For too long, we have labeled people as wicked or good, never realizing how often those two worlds collide. We are neither one nor the other! We are sometimes both. Or neither! But the point is, we need to work together to survive and keep Enchantasia safe."

"Says the girl who practically destroyed the royal court," I mutter to myself.

"Devin!" Prue jogs up to me with a fairy girl in an FTRS uniform. "Have you seen Tara? I haven't seen her since she was with Clarissa, and Headmaster Pierce was asking about her." She looks around worriedly. "You don't think she ditched Charmed to Meet You, do you?"

"No, not that I'd blame her, but she knows it's mandatory to stay." I spin around, shielding my eyes from the sun to see if I can spot her. I don't. Students are running in every direction, and a few magic carpets zoom past my head as a gnome yells about the rug going off-track. Where is she? And come to think of it... "Hey. Have you seen Anna?"

"No." Prue scratches her glittery chin. "Now that you mention it, I lost sight of her when Emerson stopped us at the field to try to get interviews for *HEAS*. Should we try looking for them?"

"Devin!" Emerson waves to me from the poison-apple booth. "Could you come here?"

Uh-oh. I quickly spin Prue around. "That's a great idea. Let's split up. I'll check the corn maze; you check the magic carpets, then we'll meet back at the beanstalks."

Prue jogs off in one direction while I go in the other toward the corn maze. It's only when I can no longer hear Emerson calling me that I slow down.

Geese swoop over my head. *Storm coming! Storm coming! Danger!*

There's still not a cloud in the sky. I don't get what they're talking about, but I do hear talking and the voices are familiar.

"This is none of your business! I don't even know you!"

"And I don't know you either, but I still know when someone needs help."

I inch around the back of the corn maze and see two figures' shoes. One is wearing boots; the other is wearing very muddy boots.

"As if I'd take your help? You almost erased the kingdom! At least I never did that."

Tara.

"Well, now I'm trying to save it."

Anna.

I sneak closer.

"Devin, where are you?" Emerson calls.

I slip around the corner and come face-to-face with Tara and Anna.

"Devin!" they say at the same time. Both look startled.

"Hi," I say casually. "Everyone is looking for you two. Again."

They look at each other. "We're fine." Anna throws an arm around Tara, who stiffens. "We teamed up and somehow got lost in the corn maze. We were just arguing over how to get out."

"You are out." I motion to the maze wall, which we are all outside of.

"Oh! Really?" Anna's eyes are as round as teacup saucers. "Look at that! Go, team!" She holds up her hand to high-five Tara, but Tara just looks at her.

"My head is killing me," Tara says.

"Are you okay?" I ask as she pulls at her head, which is covered in several braids again.

"Yeah. I get like this when it's going to storm. I think I need to lie down. Sorry, Anna, you're going to need a new partner." Tara brushes past me.

"Tara?" I try, going after her, but she's really fast and I'm blinded by the sun in my eyes. It's not going to rain! What is everyone talking about?

"Leave her. She certainly doesn't want to talk to you," Anna says.

I whirl around. "And she'd want to talk to you?"

"I'm not the one trying to bail on school," Anna says triumphantly and my face falls. "Oh yeah, I know all about you wanting to ditch RA and go to Nottingham."

"How do you know that?" I ask suspiciously. "Were you the one who left me that school pamphlet?"

"Pamphlet? What pamphlet? I hear things," Anna says. "And I also get what Tara is going through. And right now, Tara needs space." Her face softens. "But she also needs help. Listen…"

"My friends and I can help Tara just fine without you meddling," I snip. "Just stay away from her. Stay away from all of us."

Anna's face hardens. "With pleasure!"

I storm back around the corn maze, wondering why I came over here in the first place. Then I see Emerson again. For the love of Grimm, she's everywhere!

"There you are!" she says, taking my arm and practically lifting me into the air. "And your little roommate too!" She grabs Anna with her other free hand. "Great! You two are the last ones I need for the group magic-carpet race. *Happily Ever After Scrolls* is going to cover the whole thing. Come along."

Anna and I look at each other and reluctantly follow.

STORMY SKIES

O h good, you found them!" Snow says happily.

Snow is standing at the start of the magic carpet track alongside Headmistress Flora, Headmaster Pierce, a *HEAS* reporter, a few ogres and goblins I don't recognize, and my friends. Behind them is a crowd of FTRS and RA kids watching the racetrack, which is still being tested by gnomes. I watch a bright-blue oriental rug do a back flip in the air and come to a stop in front of Snow. It's the largest racing carpet I've ever seen.

"Ready for a ride?" Heath teases me.

"Meet your team," Emerson says, motioning to Heath, Raina, and two boys in FTRS uniforms, one a dark-skinned boy wearing a pirate bandanna and the other a troll who towers over him and has a gold earring dangling from his left ear. Neither look thrilled about this situation. "Wait. Where is the other one? Raina?"

"Here." My roommate emerges from the crowd, holding up the hem of her lace-trimmed dress and looking rather unhappy. She turns to her sister. "You know I'm not the best flyer, even when I'm inside a carriage with a skilled Pegasus taking us somewhere! Now you want me on an open-air carpet?"

Snow places a cool hand over her sister's. "You'll be fine, Raina. We need you to step up." She eyes the crowd. "Show everyone how working together is done."

"And on the other team," Headmaster Pierce reads from a scroll handed to him from Emerson, "we have Anna Cobbler and Tyson Bennett from Fairy Tale Reform School and our very own Sasha Briarwood from Royal Academy."

Sasha frowns. "Why do we have fewer people?"

"I'll go. I've never ridden a carpet before," Corden volunteers, slipping out of the crowd. It's the first time I've seen him today, and I can't help noticing how cool the silver eyeshadow he's wearing is paired with the dark liner under his eyes.

"Great," Sasha deadpans. "Any other takers? We should have five like Heath's team."

"Or we could stick with four so we don't drag the weight of the carpet down," Anna points out. "We'll go faster that way."

Sasha thinks about this. "Hmm…on second thought…"

A cardinal swoops by my head, and people shriek as it poops and a white substance drips onto a boy's uniform. *Stay on the ground, Devin! It's going to be stormy out there! Danger!*

I look up in surprise, but the cardinal is gone before I can ask it anything. Still no clouds anywhere. I look over. Anna is staring at me strangely. I look away.

"You know the rules," Headmistress Flora says. "Stick to the course—and *only* the course! Whoever reaches the end first wins…" She turns to Snow. "What exactly do they win?"

"Bragging points, of course," says Rose, jumping in. "I've been tallying the scores all day, and Fairy Tale Reform School is beating Royal Academy by six points." There is a cheer from the Fairy Tale Reform School kids.

"We can't have that now, can we?" Heath says.

Snow's pale forehead furrows. "I didn't realize we were making this a competition. Aren't we trying to unite the children?"

"Competition is good!" Rose argues.

"Not when we're pitting the schools against each other," Snow tries. "I thought they were teaming up to…"

I tune them out and stare out at the racecourse. It goes over two hills and around the corn maze, skirting the edge of the Hollow Woods that are still smoking in the distance. I can see Fairy Tale Reform School's turrets far off to my right and a construction crane. There is the sound of hammering behind me as the ELF Construction crew continues to work on replacing the ballroom roof. Overhead I see a few ELF Construction Pegasi carriages carrying materials through the sky from one school to the other. Construction Pegasi are still the only ones allowed in the sky. I see no clouds, but I can't help worrying. Animals have never steered me wrong before. Should we be staying on the ground?

"Excuse me," I interrupt Snow and Rose. "Is it safe to fly? I'm hearing it's going to rain. Plus, there is all this construction going on in the zone. What if one of our carpets connects with one of the Pegasi carriages?"

Rose dismisses me with a wave of her hand. "Won't happen. The carpets are programmed to stay much lower to the ground for your safety. Just steer around the construction and you'll be fine. Plus, there isn't a cloud in the sky!"

I notice Anna staring at me again. "But this cardinal just told me…"

"Devin," Emerson's smile is tight as she whispers in my ear. "We told *HEAS* we would have a magic carpet race for them to cover for the lead story. Please don't cause a scene. Just fly. You'll be back in ten minutes." She grabs my arm. "And sit like a lady, please, and tuck your dress under your knees like Raina so we don't show the world your bloomers."

I want to point out I'm wearing pants, but why bother? "Okay," I say instead as we march over to the carpets to get on. I can hear a ringing in my ears, and the hairs on the back of my neck are standing up as a sudden breeze whips across the field. Are the animals right about this storm?

"Team A!" Rose calls Anna's group over to the blue ornamental carpet. They climb aboard and the carpet bucks slightly. "This one is a bit restless—hasn't flown in weeks—so hold on tight and take a quick trial lap while we load up Team B." Corden waves as he helps direct the carpet off the ground. I hear the group give a collective scream that turns into a laugh as they disappear, Anna's brown hair flapping in the breeze.

"Team B!" Rose announces, and we walk over to a green carpet that is bucking more than the blue one was. Rose tries to hold it down. "Stop it! You agreed to participate!" she argues with the rug. "Sorry. Green hasn't been out since the battle, and I think he's still a bit worked up about—*oof!*" One of the rug's yellow tassels smacks Rose in the face and I snort. "Just get on, will you?"

I pet the edge of the carpet, thinking of it like a Pegasi or any anxious creature I've worked on. "Hey there, Green," I say softly. "I'm Devin Nile. Sorry about the commotion and all the riders about to climb onboard. Wasn't our choice." The rug starts to calm. "I promise the ride will be quick, okay? And we'll stick to the course. You'll be back in no time and then hopefully you can lounge on one of the school patios or in a pretty office and not have to fly again for a while. Sound good?" One of the tassels rises up to caress my cheek. *Score.* "Everyone on!" I say to the others.

"Nice," Heath says. "But I get to steer."

"You can try," I tell him as I climb on and help Raina up. The FTRS kids climb onto the back, trying to sit as far away from us they can.

The troll looks a little green. "I'm not sure about this. I think I'm going to be sick. Yes. Definitely sick." He starts to gag.

"You can do it!" The other boy pats him on the back. "Don't leave me on here with them alone."

The troll makes a retching noise and I spring across the carpet, quickly leaning his head over the side where he tosses his oatmeal.

"Okay, he doesn't have to ride," Rose agrees, wrinkling her nose as Heath helps the troll off. "Team A only has four, so I guess it's fine. Take a practice lap and be gone already."

Settled back in, Heath moves to the front edge of the carpet. "Ready?" He claps the FTRS kid still with us on the back, and the boy looks at him in surprise. "Let's take this carpet up! Floor it, Green!"

The carpet moves with a jolt, taking to the sky as everyone on the ground cheers.

"I thought I was driving!" I complain.

Heath looks back at me as the wind whips his curls. His eyes are distinctly blue. "You didn't say anything about the test track. Green, let's see what you've got!" He pats the carpet, and the rug takes off, flying so fast that Raina screams. We zip around the track so quickly we lap Anna and take another turn, which causes them to shout something from their own carpet, but I can't hear. We glide along, up and over hills marked with tiny floating FTRS and RA flags to mark the route.

While we can't fly as high as we normally could, I can

still see most of Enchantasia from this height and things look relatively normal. No smoke. No sign of storm clouds anywhere, not even over the mountain ridge. And no sign of destruction from the Battle of Rumpelstiltskin. For a moment, I let myself imagine things are fine and I'm waving goodbye to my family and heading to Nottingham where there is no Emerson Emet making me do interviews and I don't have to worry about sitting properly on a carpet. Do Heath or the FTRS boy look concerned about their flying appearance? No.

Even though things here have supposedly changed, I know deep down it will take more than a few decrees to make a difference in how the kingdom views royals versus nonroyals. Just the thought of how long that debate could go on is enough to make me want to take a nap. Thankfully, the cool air keeps me awake and focused on the track ahead. It twists and turns and has one or two stunt moves—over a floating rope and through a flashing cloud-made tunnel—but it's truly harmless. Maybe this won't be as bad as I thought. I can see the finish line ahead. I am ready to glide right into it and take the reins from Heath when I hear a commotion from behind me and a loud popping sound.

"Hey! Is their carpet smoking?" Heath asks as we watch Anna, Corden, Tyson, and Sasha's carpet start to rock back and forth. *Bang! Whiz!* "And are those wand flares?"

It's definitely wand work! Someone on the carpet is aiming at them or at each other. I can hear shouting and Sasha is waving frantically to us, trying to say something I can't hear.

"Fly closer!" I instruct Heath just as Anna's carpet takes off like a shot. It veers off course and practically collides with an ELF Construction carriage, which plummets fast to avoid a collision. "After them!" I cry, rushing up behind Heath to help him steer just as an alarm sounds.

Pop! A mirror appears in the sky, of all places, and the glass swirls with gray, blue, and green. "Warning! You are violating the rules of the Charmed to Meet You event," booms Milo's voice. "All students must stay on the course. Please head back to the starting line and—"

BOOM!

Anna and Sasha's carpet collides with the mirror. It smashes to the ground as their carpet flies by, Sasha still calling to us.

"*Go!*" I cry, my heart thumping as I wonder what's going on.

"Are you crazy?" Raina and Tyson, the boy from FTRS, say at the same time. They look at one another before grabbing each other's hands.

Heath and I barrel forward, each taking a front tassel to steer. Green doesn't argue with us. He turns sharply right and follows the blue carpet before it can become a dot in the distance. We tail it as it flies around the Fairy Tale Reform School turrets, up and under a construction crane, and then sideways toward the Hollow Woods.

Anna. She's looking for something. Or someone.

"Olivina!" I cry over the sound of the wind whipping past us as our carpet moves at warp speed. "Anna must know where she is! She's trying to hand Sasha and Corden over to her!"

"Are you sure?" Heath shouts.

"Positive!" I say even though I'm not. My heart is thumping in my chest. Anna disappearing. Talking to Tara. Maybe she misses villain work and is trying to get in league with a new villain. That's the only explanation. "Follow her to the—"

"*Duck!*" Raina and Tyson scream as our carpet almost collides with something midair.

Heath and I dive just in time. I turn back to see what it

was, but it's already flapping off in the other direction, its hairy, huge wings soaring into a nearby cloud.

"What was that?" Raina cries.

Was that a dragon? A harpy? A firebird?

Help us! Please!

Someone is calling to me. I look around the sky for a cardinal or geese in trouble.

Help us! They've found us! Please!

"Devin!" Heath is shaking me. "Help me steer."

"Here comes another one!" Tyson cries out as we almost hit a gray creature head on.

It screeches, and I see fangs, smell the stench, and immediately recoil. "Gargoyles!" I cry. The minions of Rumpelstiltskin and Alva and most likely Olivina. What are they doing here?

"Heath! One is coming right at us!" Raina screams as it flies by our side.

Heath and I both lean to the right and pull the tassels.

"Hang on!" I cry, but then I hear the voices again.

Help us! Please!

I look over. A big gargoyle and a small one are flying alongside us now, and if I'm not mistaken, they are looking at me.

Help! Help! Please help us!

I grab my head. Their voices can't be the ones I am hearing. Magical creature caretakers can't hear animals that are evil. It's one of the most basic rules. It's why I never heard the harpies. It's why I had trouble communicating with the firebird who, while not necessarily evil, wasn't friendly either. It's why I've never tried talking to a sea serpent or a mountain troll. They're not on the side of good. I let go of the carpet and hold my head.

"Devin, are you okay?" Heath shouts. "Devin? Hang on! I'm calling for the royal guard." He taps an SOS signal on his mini magical scroll. "They'll take to the air on Pegasi in seconds if the transmission goes through," Heath tells us. "We just have to hold on till then."

"What about Sasha and Corden?" Raina cries. "We have to get to them. If Anna is trying to hand them over to Olivina, we have to stop her. Devin? Devin?"

But I'm not listening to Raina. All I can think about are the gargoyles. Why would I hear them? I'm not evil. They are! I shake my head. I need to focus. Our friends need us. Forget the gargoyles. "I'm fine. Just a headache," I tell Raina, Heath, and Tyson. "Just try to find Anna. We can't let her get away with Sasha and Corden."

"Trying," Heath says as he steers Green over another dark cloud. "It's getting hard to see."

"There's definitely a storm coming," says Tyson nervously. "And I don't want to be in the air when it hits."

"We can't land without the others," I say determinedly. "Keep going!"

Whiz! Boom!

The carpet goes sideways and everyone screams.

I turn around and see flames crackling through the sky and a flurry of smoke. A group of Pegasi are heading our way, rising out of the dark clouds that are suddenly forming around us.

"It's the royal guard!" Raina says. "We're saved! Over here! Help us!"

BOOM!

Another blast rocks the carpet.

"They're firing at the good guys!" Heath shouts. "What are they doing?"

"They can't see," I realize, "and we're surrounded by gargoyles." Another flame shoots out from a wand and I know it's headed our way. "Green! *Dive!*"

Green drops fast, gliding in and out of clouds, but several

gargoyles are still on our tail. I hold on tight again and focus on Anna's carpet straight ahead. Several gargoyles have surrounded it too. Suddenly, Anna's blue carpet pulls out in front and turns around to face us. She's shouting, Sasha's shouting, but I can't understand what they're saying over all this wind whipping up.

Please! He's only a baby! Save him! Save him, girl! I know you can hear me!

I look at the creature flying next to me. It's the ugliest, foulest creature I've ever seen. It has rancid breath, huge claws, and fangs that are dripping foam from its mouth. Its eyes are bright yellow and its skin black and hairy with wings that could cut our carpet down with one fell swoop. Instead it flaps alongside us, never getting too close or too far. I'm so confused, I don't even know what to say. Then, under the large creature's wing, I see it—a small, slightly less hairy creature, lighter gray in color with big, wide eyes that are positively terrified.

Just take him! If you can't help me, take him!

I hold my ears again, trying to block her out. I'm not evil. Am I? No, I'm not! This is Olivina's trickery! I shouldn't be hearing any of this, and suddenly I'm angry at the thought of her out there, nearby, pulling the strings as she's done for far too long. "Who do you work for?" I shout at the creature. "Where is Olivina? Take us to her!"

Raina tugs on the back of my dress. "Devin! What are you doing? Don't talk to gargoyles!"

Whiz! Another flame shoots past us and then what appears to be a poison apple.

"HALT! By order of the royal guard!" I hear someone shout, but the fog is growing so thick, I can't see anywhere off our carpet.

"Stop!" Heath cries. "There are students up here! Hold your fire!" He tries to turn the carpet around. Tyson and Raina both start to panic. "Devin! Help me call to them!"

The little gargoyle starts squeaking in fear. I can feel my heart pounding out of my chest as the thunder booms, growing closer as the clouds seem to thicken like pea soup. They shroud Anna's carpet from us. Flares flash, the sound of booms continues, and I feel Green diving and leaping through the clouds, trying to draw closer to the royal guard.

"Stop it!" I suddenly hear a voice scream. "You're scaring them! They've done nothing wrong!"

It's Anna, and she's flown up beside us.

"*Help us!*" Sasha screams as much to me as she does to the royal guard drawing closer. I can still see the gargoyles through the smoke and flames, staying just ahead of the royal guard and their Pegasi. The mother nearest to me looks at me again.

You can save him! Please!

But I just stare at her, not knowing what to do.

Whiz! A flame shoots between me and the gargoyle and hits it in its left wing. The creature starts to free-fall.

"*No!*" Anna cries, diving after it. I see all their faces, wrapped in terror as they disappear into the clouds.

"Follow her!" I shout without thinking and pull on the tassel. The royal guard dives after us.

We descend so fast, I'm not sure what's happening. Everyone is shouting, and I can't see the gargoyle anymore or Anna's carpet. Forget the gargoyles. I have to get to my friends.

"Devin!" Raina cries. "We're going to hit the ground!"

But I continue to steer Green downward, trying in vain to catch the blue carpet.

Heath pulls up at the last second and we bump along, hitting a tree, and then a bush before crashing into a pile of leaves in the forest. "Is everyone all right?"

"Where is the other carpet?" I cry, jumping off Green.

The royal guard land behind us. "Don't move, villains!" one of the guards' shouts. "Don't move or we'll shoot!"

Two wounded gargoyles come crawling out of the brush, one dripping blood. Anna appears out of nowhere and dives in front of them.

"No, please! They're innocent! Don't hurt them!"

"I found the others!" Tyson calls. "They're hurt but they're alive! They're over here!"

The others go running, but my eyes are still on the gargoyles, looking badly beaten and doing nothing to get away.

The royal guards throw a net over the creatures, which electrifies and zaps them.

"*No!*" Anna cries. "Stop!" Her eyes lock on me. "Devin, do something! They have a baby! Didn't you hear them? They said, 'Help us!' They need our help! Tell them what you heard!"

Everyone is looking at me.

"No," I say, backing up, shaking my head.

Anna is evil. I am not. I couldn't have heard. It was all in my head. "I didn't hear anything."

GIFTED

I stick with my story. When the headmasters from FTRS and RA call us up to the office to talk about what happened on the magic carpet racetrack, I keep my mouth shut and let others do the talking as much as I can. Thankfully, they're preoccupied with Raina since she gave an interview to the *Happily Ever After Scrolls* reporters before Emerson could whisk us away.

Now Emerson is doing damage control, Sasha is furious she's been scooped when she was actually part of the race herself (and swears she's going to be up all night writing her own firsthand account), and the headmasters have vowed to shut down all outdoor activities except ones where we're being supervised by the royal guard. Apparently they will be patrolling the grounds 24/7 now.

"It's like we're in prison," Prue says as she looks out the window of the headmasters' office.

"I'm sorry, but it's for everyone's safety," Snow says, keeping an arm around a distraught Raina. She looks at me again worriedly. "Are you sure there is nothing else any of you have to add about the gargoyles?"

"No," we all say again.

I do my best to avoid making eye contact.

"Miss Cobbler from Fairy Tale Reform School swears she could hear the gargoyles asking for help," Pierce mentions again. "She's been with the FTRS teachers for over an hour and she insists the gargoyles weren't trying to harm any of you, but no one has backed up her claims."

I feel my face warm and will it not to. *I did not hear the gargoyles. I did not hear the gargoyles.*

"Good can't hear evil," Heath says simply. "Everyone knows that. Those beasties were out for blood, and we were caught in the middle. We were just trying to survive with the royal guard using us as target practice."

"That won't happen again," Snow says sternly. "I appreciate

you alerting the royal guard, but they went a little too far with their tactics when we had students in the crosshairs. I'm just thankful none of you were hurt."

"I am never riding a carpet again." Raina sniffs.

"Neither am I," Logan agrees. He's still wrapped in the blanket the nurse at the infirmary gave him when they checked us out post-attack. "And I never want to see one of those nasty beasties again. In fact, I am investing in a radish farm so I can arm myself against the creatures in case we ever cross paths in the future. Don't you think that's a good defense, Devin?"

"What? Yeah. Great," I say, because truthfully all I can think about is what Anna might be saying about me during her questioning next door.

I notice Pierce and Snow looking at each other. "It's been a long night. Why don't you all retire and get some sleep?" Snow suggests.

But I can't sleep. Even after Raina offers me one of her aromatherapy sleep masks, I lie there for hours thinking about the gargoyles and what I did—or didn't—hear. At some point I fall asleep, but then I'm up again before the rest of the room. That's when I pull out the Nottingham brochure again and look at it longingly. (Yes, I have more than one. When

Snow took mine, I asked Dimitri to fly to Nottingham and get me a new one.)

Over 300 animal language course offerings! Learn how to communicate with everyone from the smallest fire ant to krakens!

- Work with our rehabilitation team to reintroduce dragons and wyvern to the wild!
- Train to survive for a year in the woods with nothing but your own well-honed animalistic instincts!
- Learn how to mix ingredients for holistic animal treatments from esteemed herbologist Venus Flytrap!

And study creature caretaking under the very best in the business. You won't be disappointed when you attend Nottingham School for Nature and Wild Beasts!

Nottingham sounds like exactly what I need.

Too bad I'll never get there.

"I know you heard them!" Anna hisses in my ear, and I jump when I realize she's standing over my bed. "Why can't you just admit it?"

I cram the brochure under my pillow and pull Anna into the quiet hallway. Most of the castle isn't up yet. A member of the ELF Cleaning crew hired to dust during the construction is cleaning windows in the hallway.

"I didn't hear anything!" I whisper-shout back to her. "I'm not evil!"

"And neither are they!" Anna counters. Her face crumbles. "I think they just wanted our help. And you let the royal guard shoot them out of the sky!"

"I had nothing to do with the royal guard shooting them! But I wasn't helping gargoyles either, just like you shouldn't, if you're trying to be as good as you claim to be." I look around to make sure the ELF crew can't hear us. "You know gargoyles worked for Alva just like you did! You can't trust them!"

"But these were asking for help," Anna says, sounding agitated. "I heard it. I know I did. I've been around a lot of gargoyles, obviously, and I've never heard them speak to me before. Maybe they were tricked into helping villains just like I was."

I snort. "You don't look like someone who could be tricked."

Anna rolls her eyes. "Fine. Brainwashed. My point is, they could be innocent, but you won't take the time to help me find out."

"No, I won't!" I hiss. "Keep me out of your plans. I couldn't hear the gargoyles. If you did, then maybe you're the one who needs help." She flinches and for a moment I feel bad. "Look, all I care about is finding Olivina and getting out of this school once and for all. Now if you excuse me, I have to get ready for class."

"Devin!" Anna hurries after me, but I'm done listening.

Instead I hear a peck, peck, peck at the window. I stop short and Anna practically slams into my back. It's Dimitri.

Oh, Devin! Thank goodness I found you. We just found a family of raccoons that were living in a hollowed-out log. They were injured in the battle and need help but couldn't make it this far—not with all the construction. You need to come right away.

My heart lurches. *I can't,* I chirp. *We're forbidden to leave the castle, but I'll put together a first aid kit in my room for you to bring them. Maybe if I give instructions, you'll know what to do. I'll be right back!* I start back for our bedroom.

"Are you really going to send this dove to help them when you're the one they need?" Anna snaps.

I spin around. "You understood that?"

Anna scratches her head, looking confused herself. "I think so…" She points to the dove. "He said a family of hurt raccoons are living in a hollowed-out log, and then you said, 'I can't leave school grounds.' Which is ridiculous when you're needed, but am I right?"

She's a creature caretaker too? Dimitri chirps.

No! Is she? I open my mouth and close it. How did Anna do that? I don't know anyone at school other than Snow who can communicate with animals like I can. "Have you had creature caretaker training?"

Anna shakes her head, but suddenly she looks excited. "I've never spoken to a creature before in my life! Well, aside from yesterday! This is amazing! I knew you were a creature caretaker, but I thought you'd trained for it."

I scowl. "I have." I head to the bedroom to get Dimitri's supplies. Anna follows me.

It's probably beginner's luck or something. Anna can't have the gift I have.

"Then how am I doing it without knowing how?" Anna asks.

The rest of the room is up, getting dressed and consulting their scrolls for schedules. Sasha is the only one writing away and not paying attention to the world around her.

"Doing what?" Prue asks as she pushes her hair under the purple witch's hat she loves.

"Nothing," I say quickly.

"Talking to animals!" Anna says excited. "I just did it."

"No you didn't!" I grab a kit with herbs, bandages, and supplies small enough for Dimitri to carry. I feel awful I can't go myself, but I don't want to get in trouble. I look over at Tara's bed. It's empty. The hairs on my arms stand up. "Hey. Do you guys know where Tara is?" I glance at Anna, who immediately looks away.

"She said something about checking her schedule with Headmaster Pierce before class," Raina says. "I told her she should stop at the infirmary after. She looks awful. Dreadful under-eye bags. If anyone needs a spa day, it's Tara."

"She's always been a restless sleeper," Prue explains. "And she's always been up before dawn and out the door. But since we got here, it seems worse. Sometimes I look over and she's not even in bed in the middle of the night. She's just pacing."

"Lily swears she saw Tara sleepwalking," I say. "Have any of you?" They shake their heads.

"I'm sure she's fine," Anna says. "What we should really be talking about is me. I can speak to animals! Devin saw me do it!"

"No you didn't!" I say again, getting aggravated.

"I did too!" Anna glares at me as Dimitri flutters to the next window to wait for his instructions. "Watch!" she tells the other roommates. She opens the window and Dimitri hops inside. "Hey there!" Anna says, cooing to the dove. "I'm Anna. What's your name?"

"It doesn't work like that," I say as the others gather around to watch.

Dimitri! the dove says.

"Dimitri!" Anna says triumphantly and turns to me, looking smug. "See?"

"Whoa," Sasha says, looking up from her parchment. "I thought that was Devin's gift!"

"It is," I argue.

"Didn't you train forever?" Raina asks.

"I did!" I reply, my blood boiling as Anna continues to look pretty pleased with herself.

"I thought it was hard," Prue adds.

"It is!"

"Then how am I doing it?" Anna asks. "And how can I hear a good creature like a dove but also a so-called bad one like a gargoyle? Just like you did?"

Raina gasps. "You heard the gargoyles?"

"I didn't hear anything!" I grab one of my simplest dresses and hurry behind the dressing partition to change. Who does Anna Cobbler think she is, coming into my life and trying to act like she knows how to talk to creatures? We are nothing alike. Nothing! And yet...

"Morning, students!" Milo's voice echoes through the room as I come around the other side of the partition and see our mirror turning magenta. "This morning is your first day of new classes, so we hope you've all consulted your scrolls for both location and timing. We don't want to be late!"

"Absolutely not, Milo," Miri says as the mirror turns peach. "Thank you for reminding the students to be punctual."

The mirror turns orange. "My pleasure, Miri. You've taught me well."

"Oh, stop!" The mirror turns pink. "You've taught me so much too!"

"You've taught me more!"

"No, you have!" Miri says with a giggle.

"Are our mirrors flirting?" Sasha asks.

Miri clears her throat. "But anyway, our point is, be on time and enjoy your new classes. Most are here at Royal Academy, but there are a few at FTRS as well. Please leave extra time to get there."

"And remember, royal guard members are on the grounds today still investigating yesterday's incident. For your safety, they will be overseeing all travel between schools and combing the grounds. All students are asked to stay indoors—unless they are scheduled to be elsewhere. Thank you and have a great day!"

"Oooh! My first class today is Pretty in Ink: How Calligraphy and the Handwritten Message Can Uplift a Kingdom," Raina says.

"Hey, I have that too," Sasha says.

"Me three," says Prue, looking at her scroll. "Devin?"

My scroll glows and comes to life, revealing my schedule. "My first class is Magical Creature Care at Fairy Tale Reform School with Princess Dragonfly." At least it's a good class.

"Ooh! I heard my sister talking about Princess Dragonfly," Raina says. "Apparently she's super-qualified and had the best teaching recommendations. Snow hired her on the spot."

"I guess we'll see if that's true. I have class with her too." Anna shows us her scroll.

Great.

Sasha avoids a smirk, but just barely. "I guess you two should head over there together."

This day just keeps getting better and better.

WHAT'S SO MAGICAL
ABOUT THAT?

To leave the castle, there's now a bag check by the royal guards. They question everything from a compact to the small bottle of herbs I carry on me in case we run into a creature that's gotten into poison ivy. (It happens more than you think.) Anna is stopped because she has a bag with all kinds of fruit in it.

"I have low blood sugar. I have to eat often," she tells him and he lets it go.

A few items are confiscated, and anyone carrying a wand has to have it labeled and locked up in a special carriage compartment until the end of the ride. After a half hour of checks and questioning, we're finally allowed to take off into the sky. The driver says our ride should be about fifteen minutes long.

That's fine by me. I don't know anyone other than Anna among the mix of RA and FTRS students in the carriage. Most are quiet, which is good, and I need the time to calm down. I can't believe Anna can communicate with animals! Without training! And how is she able to talk to good and evil creatures? Have I been wrong about this good/evil creature rule the entire time? It's not like I've had any formal training myself. I'm self-taught, which is why I need Nottingham!

"Hey! I know you!" a Royal Academy girl in a peach confection says to Anna. "Aren't you Anna Cobbler?"

Anna looks up from the book she's reading on creature migration patterns. "What about it?" she says, her voice even.

"Your sister is Gilly, right? OMG, I just read in *Happily Ever After Scrolls* that she is receiving the Medal of Magical Honor for her bravery in the Battle of Rumpelstiltskin."

"That's *huge!*" says the boy next to her, who has the puffiest pompadour I've ever seen. "The royal court has only given that out once before—to Red Riding Hood. Your sister must be a big deal."

"Yep," Anna says with a small sigh. "Everyone loves Gilly."

For a moment, I feel bad. I'm an only child so I wouldn't know, but I heard Anna tell Prue she's one of several kids living in a crowded boot. It's got to be hard living in the shadow of a famous sibling.

"Yeah, but the kingdom doesn't love you," one of the Fairy Tale Reform School kids says, and a few others laugh.

"At least people have heard of me," Anna says with a nasty smile.

Within minutes, we're landing at Fairy Tale Reform School. Everyone looks out the windows to see what remains of the school. Parts of the grounds nearby are still smoking and the turret nearest us is charred black, with part of the roof missing. Several windows in the nearby building are broken and one of the wings is reduced to rubble, while several others have extensive damage.

"Whoa! Half the castle is gone!"

"I thought they rebuilt it with a golden egg."

"Yeah, but the effects were short-lived and some of the stuff started shrinking after a few days. Some of the kids got stuck in tiny dorm rooms and had to be magically removed."

As we exit the carriage, I can see there are ELF Construction crews everywhere, and the sound of hammering and yelling directions is overwhelming. How could anyone concentrate? No wonder they can't hold school here.

"So why is it safe for us to take class here?" I ask as a dragonfly zips past us.

"Because you're with me!" says the dragonfly as it transforms in front of our eyes into a tall, wiry woman in a black dress with a skirt that looks like an intricate web. Her large, oval eyes are a glittery yellow, reminding me of an insect.

"Whoa!" says an FTRS boy as the rest of us clap, impressed.

"I'm Princess Dragonfly, and I'm new to Enchantasia, having recently transplanted from Nottingham where I was a teacher at the School for Nature and Wild Beasts."

I stand up straighter. *Wait. My future school?*

The girl in the peach dress sniffs the air. "Does anyone else smell chocolate?"

Princess Dragonfly laughs. "Oh, that would be me! My signature scent, I'm afraid. Masks the insect odor I sometimes have. I hope none of you mind."

We all shake our heads.

"Your teachers at both schools needed some help with all you've had going on, you poor things. As I am an expert in creature/human transformation—an upper-level skill—and handling magical creatures as tiny as an ant and as large as a leviathan—which I have ridden at least a half-dozen times—I was the right teacher for the job. So come along!" she says, ushering us down a path marked with caution tape. "Let's go talk about magical creatures, shall we?"

I am the first one behind her. "Hi! I'm Devin Nile," I say, extending my hand to grasp her thin, bony one. "I'm a magical creature caretaker. At least I'm studying to be one, and I'm dying to go to your school in Nottingham and train further. Right now I can speak squirrel, several varieties of waterfowl, and am practically fluent in zebra and giraffe, although I've never met either. But I have gone toe to toe with a firebird."

"It's lovely to meet you, Devin," she says, shaking my hand. "And who's this?" she asks as the next student waits for their turn to greet her.

That's okay she has to move on. I'm more than ready to impress her with my skills in creature care, and I don't have to wait that long to do it. She whisks us off to what she explains was the one area of the castle that wasn't damaged in the Battle of Rumpelstiltskin—the dungeon—which is where some student named Maxine Hockler bravely began transporting caged creatures so they could survive the battle. And they all did.

"They've since been joined by several dozen more creatures from as near as Royal Academy and as far away as the village, who were injured during the battle and the destruction following," Princess Dragonfly says. She holds up a blue jay wearing slings on both wings. "It is our job to care for these creatures till they are ready to be reintroduced to the kingdom."

There is a distinct smell in the dungeons, which have been transformed into a pet shelter of sorts with cages big and small set up in sections. I spot two elephants, a tiger that has been given a cell all to himself, three unicorns, almost a dozen deer, and small woodland creatures. There are oversize parrot cages with birds suffering from post-battle anxiety and a group of small dogs that bark anytime there is the sound of hammering (which happens every five seconds). Between all the neighs, barks, moos, hisses, and baas, it's quite loud. And that's just in the regular section of the dungeon. There are also magical creatures housed in another room that Princess Dragonfly says have been trained to choose students to make "their pets" as part of a program the school runs.

"But you won't be participating in that right now," she says. "Right now our job is to keep these creatures safe and well fed and attend to their needs." She sits down at a tidy desk that has nothing but a quill and a piece of parchment on it. "I want you to walk around and get a feeling for the creatures that need our aid. Don't worry about treatment yet. For now, use your emotions to guide you. What do these creatures need? What do they want?"

Everyone in the group shuffles off to explore the cages. The girl in the peach dress talks to the unicorns while the snide boy is fond of the tiger, who looks like he wants to eat him. Princess Dragonfly observes each student, not saying much, which makes it my perfect chance to impress her.

"Princess?" I ask as she fixes the top knot she has her hair in. "Where are your lizards and reptiles? I have a bearded dragon for a pet and speak reptile really well, so I think I'd be a great help with them."

"That's wonderful, Devin, but if you can already do that well, don't you think you should focus on something you *don't* do well?" she asks as the smell of chocolate radiating off her puts me in a happy state. "I'm not interested in students who want to show off the skills they already know. I want to help you learn new ones!"

I falter and feel my cheeks begin to burn. "I wasn't trying to show off. I just—"

"Wow! How did she do that?"

"Did you see that? She got him to go to sleep!"

There is a commotion in the next section, and Princess Dragonfly leaves me to see what's going on. I follow. Anna is standing in front of the elephant cage with the rest of the class behind her. She's kneeling in front of the bars whispering to the baby elephant who is letting her pet him as he snores.

"What's this?" Princess Dragonfly asks.

Anna whirls around. "The baby was crying, and I felt bad so I started talking to it in a soft voice, saying everything would be okay and how it probably needed a nap, and it finally lay down and closed its eyes! I think it said it wanted me to stay by it while it slept." She bites her lower lip. "I think it even said its name is Ronald."

Princess Dragonfly beams. "It is Ronald! How impressive! What's your name?"

"Anna," she says with a smile. "Anna Cobbler."

"And do you speak elephant?"

"No." Anna shakes her head. "I've never spoken to a creature...before this week. I didn't even know I could."

"What skill! To be able to use your human voice to speak with it, and not know elephant yet... Well, that is an upper-level skill indeed! And such a smart move, approaching a creature you've never encountered before," she adds, looking impressed.

I feel my face grow hotter.

Princess Dragonfly touches Anna's shoulder. "I can't wait to see what you do in this class. Speaking of which, let's all go over some rules in the next room. Follow me…"

The class follows after her, and I brush past Anna, who is watching me. Maybe she thinks I'll compliment her or say something about the elephant, but I can't even form words. Beginner's luck. I'm sure that's what it is. But then I feel guilty. Would it kill me to compliment her?

I turn around just in time to see Anna slipping up the stairs and out the dungeon doors. I don't hesitate. I follow.

SNEAKING AROUND

Having spent the last few years caring for woodland creatures, I've become an expert at walking through brush without being seen or heard. The trick, as my bunny friend Henri once explained, is to plant your foot from your heel to your toe and move slowly. Go too fast and you will crunch on leaves or break a twig, and every bird in the woods will alert the animals you are there.

Slow is key, as is looking down and trying to find the softest part of the ground to walk on. Mud is always good, but I just cleaned my boots, so I'm not thrilled about the prospect. Still, I don't want to lose Anna as I watch her slip out the castle doors, move past two ELF Construction guys eating lunch, and disappear into what's left of a cornfield on the grounds.

Where is she sneaking off to? If I had to guess, it would be to see Olivina. Why else risk annoying Princess Dragonfly, who clearly wants her to be teacher's pet? I watch her heavy sack bounce on her back as she runs, and it is all I can do to keep up with her. My heart is pounding as my mind swirls with conflicting thoughts. What if I'm walking into a trap? What if I'm about to face Olivina without backup?

But what if I'm about to put this whole villain problem to bed by following her? I keep going, alternately watching the ground beneath my feet and Anna so I don't lose sight of her brown hair.

Not once does she look back to see if she's being followed. Ha! Such a rookie move.

But when she disappears into a gap between two redwood trees into the Hollow Woods, I move too fast to catch up with her and my foot cracks a pile of twigs. *Drooping dragons. Nice one, Devin.*

Anna looks up from the bush she's kneeling at in alarm. A bunch of the fruit she had in her sack has rolled onto the dirt. There's also a bowl and a carafe of water. I knew it! She's hiding someone!

"You followed me?" Anna stands up fast to block me. "You need to leave. This is the Hollow Woods. They're dangerous. You could be eaten by a giant or a firebird."

I cross my arms, annoyed that she's even trying to tell me about the Hollow Woods. "I've faced both before and I'm not worried. But you should be." I move closer. "What are you hiding?" She blocks my path again. "Where is she?"

"She?" Anna's face clouds over.

"Olivina!" I push past her. "I know you're hiding that fairy godmother in here somewhere. Come out, come out, Fairy Godmother! You can't hide forever!" I notice the bush Anna was standing in front of is actually some sort of box covered with leaves and branches. "Found you!"

"No!" Anna cries as I rip the branches clear and come face-to-face with a tiny, wrinkly bald thing with a tiny tuft of hair on its head. What is that? A cat? It locks eyes with me and starts to wail. The sound is so high-pitched, birds fly out of the nearby trees and I hear the roar of a giant in the distance. I cover my ears as its scream rocks the forest. Finally, Anna swoops down and picks up the thing, wrapping it tightly in the blanket it was sitting on.

"It's okay, Edgar. It's okay," she says, bouncing the gray

thing up and down in her arms. The thing stops wailing and is reduced to sniffles. It peeks out of the blanket and looks at me suspiciously.

"What is that?" I ask, coming in to get a closer look. The tiny pointy ears, the gray color, the small wings and the tail. Its eyes are almost as big as its face. It's not hairy, and it doesn't stink, but there is no other explanation. "Is that...a baby gargoyle?"

Anna holds the creature away from me. "You can't tell anyone Edgar's here. He's just a baby!"

"I can see that," I snap as Anna pets the tiny tuff of wiry hair on its bald head. "But you can't hide him here, Anna. That thing is evil."

"No he's not! He's not even a few months old. He's an innocent."

Edgar begins to sniffle again, and I sense a wail coming so I lower my voice. "But his parents aren't. They're evil. Where are they anyway? Where is Olivina?" I walk away, looking for more gargoyles in hiding.

"I don't even know this Olivina," Anna says. "I've never met her. I only found out about Edgar last week before his parents were captured."

"So you've *still* working with gargoyles," I accuse her. "I knew it! Is Rumpelstiltskin back too? Is Alva? What else are you hiding?" Edgar wraps his tiny claws around Anna's neck.

Mama! he sobs, and Anna looks at me.

Did Edgar say 'mama'? No. It had to be the wind.

"I'm not working with the gargoyles." Anna grabs an apple from her bag and hands it to Edgar, who sniffs it, then takes a tiny bite. "I'm just trying to help them."

"Help them? Why?" This girl really does need FTRS.

"Because they're prisoners!" Anna's face crumbles. "Stiltskin's. Alva's. They worked for them because they were forced to." I roll my eyes. "It's true! Edgar's mom told me everything. At first Alva kept them in line working for her undercover in FTRS as statues, and then when they were exposed, she had them under a spell, keeping them on the side of evil. That held till the Battle of Rumpelstiltskin. When she and Stiltskin disappeared, the spell broke, and the gargoyles were free, but not really. The world thinks they're evil."

"They are," I insist.

"They've been tricked, like I was." Anna bounces Edgar on her hip. "And they know they have a lot to make up for after all the dirty deeds they've done, but they want to clear their names. They want a chance to prove they're good."

"It's too late for that. People will never trust gargoyles after everything that's happened."

Anna's eyes fill with hope. "Maybe if we help the people see what they're really like. If they can meet Edgar..."

"There is no *we*," I remind her. "I don't work with evil creatures."

"Then why can you hear him?" Anna asks and I don't respond. "And why can I hear so-called good creatures *and* evil ones? Because gargoyles are good! I'm telling you. If you just tried to talk to Edgar."

"No," I insist.

"He's sweet! I've been bringing food to his group since the battle when they went into hiding," Anna continues as if I haven't already shot her down. "They were scared after the spell lifted and upset about all they'd done. They wanted to flee Enchantasia, but with the royal guard hunting them, they had to hide, and since they knew me, they came to me for help." She raises her chin defiantly. "And that's what I've been doing. Sheltering them and bringing them food. It's harder with me at Royal Academy, and especially now when we can't get off the grounds or go outside, but I've been doing what I can." Her face crumbles.

"But then yesterday, when they saw me on the carpet, they flew up to see me. They thought I was there to bring them food, and then when the royal guard appeared…the sky started falling." She runs her free hand through her messy hair. "They were begging for help, no one would listen to me, and then that mother gargoyle was shot out of the sky holding a baby…" She chokes out a sob.

"I've heard they're okay, but they're in custody so I'm not really sure where they're being held or if they're getting treatment." She wraps her arms tighter around Edgar. "Which is why I can't let them find this guy! He's all alone now. His parents were taken away in the raid yesterday when *you* wouldn't help them."

I throw my hands up. "Reminder: they're evil!" My voice starts to rise, and Edgar starts to sob again.

"Edgar, it's okay," Anna says, making a shushing sound. "Devin is good. She loves to help creatures." Anna looks at me. "She will help us. That's what a *good* magical creature caretaker does." The baby looks over, its eyes rimmed with tears, and smiles. It's sort of creepy and cute at the same time.

I sigh. "What do you want from me, Anna?"

She hesitates. "I want you to talk to Edgar. If you can hear him, then he can't be evil, right? Because you're not evil. I kind of am, or was, so I'm not the best judge, but you're good. If you can hear him, then maybe you'll see he's an innocent and needs our help." She holds Edgar out to me. "Please? Try?"

I look at the wiggly, wrinkly thing in her arms and sigh deeper. I guess it can't hurt to *try* talking to it. "Fine. But don't expect much." I reach out for Edgar and he recoils.

"It's okay. You're safe. Go to Devin," Anna says and hands him over to me.

The two of us look at each other. He's wrinkly, but supersoft, and his large eyes remind me of a pug's. He's kind of cute. I guess. "Hey, kid. So what's the deal? Anna says you're good."

Mama, Edgar sniffs. *I want Mama.*

I heard that. I look at Anna.

"He said 'I want Mama,' right?" she asks.

I don't answer. "Edgar, do you know where Olivina is? Or Stiltskin?"

He sniffles and buries his head in my chest. *Man evil! Mama says he bad.* He looks up again, his eyes widening. *Danger. Villains still here. Danger!*

My heart stops. "Where is the danger, Edgar? Who is still here?"

Edgar won't look up. *Bad. Very bad! Want to hurt Edgar and Mama. Want to hurt people! Mama won't help. Mama...* He starts to cry softly onto my dress.

Anna and I look at each other again. There's no denying I can hear the baby. But does that mean he's good or he just hasn't turned evil yet? No one is born evil, are they? I'm so confused. This goes against all I've taught myself so far.

Which just goes to show, maybe I have more to learn about creature caretaking than I realize.

I hand Edgar back to Anna.

"Well?" she asks, but the smirk on her face says it all.

"I won't tell anyone about Edgar—for now. But you need to stop sneaking off! We'll come back together to bring Edgar supplies and food."

Anna frowns. "But what if someone finds him out here? I don't know if it's safe for him to stay in the woods."

I purse my lips. She's got a point. But what other option do we have? "We can't bring a gargoyle into school. He has to stay here till we figure this out. Maybe I can reach out to my father and find out what he knows about the gargoyles."

"Okay," Anna agrees. "Anything to keep Edgar safe." The gargoyle coos at her. "Thanks, Devin."

Wow, she said thank you. "You're welcome, but now you have to do something for me. Tell me what you were talking to Tara about the other day."

Anna's face falls. "I promised her I wouldn't."

"Is she in trouble? Is Olivina trying to reach her?"

"I don't think so." Anna hesitates. "She just needs to work through some stuff. Like we all do. And you need to give her space."

"But why?" I press, even though this sounds very Tara. She's always been a bit of an outsider by choice. "If she's in trouble, I need to know."

"She's not in trouble," Anna says carefully. "You just have to wait for her to come to you. Whether you help me with Edgar or not, I'm not spilling her secrets."

I see I've reached a dead end here. "Fine."

Anna bounces Edgar, and I think I hear him giggle. Anna smiles. "So we still have a deal?"

I look at her and the baby. "Deal."

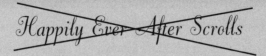
Happily Ever After Scrolls

The Enchantasia Insider

The REAL Kingdom News

GARGOYLE ATTACK AT ROYAL ACADEMY
(A FIRSTHAND ACCOUNT!)

by Sasha Briarwood

Guess what, my pretties? The rumors are true. Gargoyles have been spotted on the grounds of Royal Academy! I saw them with my own eyes!

Yes, as you've heard whispered in the Royal Underground and in the cafeteria, there was a gargoyle attack during the Charmed to Meet You event the other day. Milo and Miri may assure us there is nothing to worry about (What is going on between those two mirrors anyway?), but there is a reason the royal guard patrols our grounds now. Gargoyles are walking among us. If they're back, can Olivina or Rumpelstiltskin be far behind?

My guess? These nefarious gargoyles are scouts for the villains. They were spotted during the magic carpet race I was taking part in. One moment we were flying over the grounds, and the next, the sky was dark and stormy, and a foul stench filled the air. I heard a high-pitched squeak and turned to my left, and several of them were flying alongside our carpet, trying to poach us and bring us back to the villains.*

We tried in vain to fly away, but they flew alongside us, their hairy, grotesque bodies flapping in unison as they prepared to pounce. Their eyes were bright yellow, and their teeth more like fangs. Their claws were as long as some wands! Our group started to panic.*

Then, when I thought all hope was lost, the royal guard appeared! They shot these foul beasts out of the sky and apprehended the gargoyles. I am certain our royal guard, along with our Dwarf Police Squad, will see to it that they are fully questioned about the villains they are in league with. I, for one, will sleep better knowing these beasts are being rounded up.

*As this is my blog, this is my take on what happened. Others on my magic carpet (gargoyle sympathizers) viewed the incident differently. Stay tuned for more updates on the gargoyles and the hunt for the fairy godmother!

MIXED MAGICAL MESSAGES

S omehow, Anna and I make it back to Fairy Tale Reform School before Princess Dragonfly realizes we're missing. She's in the middle of this big speech on how unicorn blood has healing powers so we're able to sneak in the back door of the dungeon. We pretend to be convincing a cow that it needs to be milked when she looks our way.

Anna sticks to her word. Over the next few days, she doesn't say a word about Sasha's blog post calling gargoyles foul. She goes to class, doesn't argue with anyone over whose turn it is to sweep the room, and does not sneak off. I even arrange for my friend Paulo the possum to bring Edgar food and water till our next class at Fairy Tale Reform School. Things seem to be going smoothly till Emerson comes calling.

"Devin!" The fairy spots me in the hallway with Sasha on my way to a seminar called The Inner Royal: Finding the Strength Within to Lead. It's mandatory this semester.

"Is it too late to duck into a classroom and get away?" I whisper to Sasha.

"I'm just glad she's calling for you instead of me," Sasha says as we keep walking, hiding behind an ogre from Fairy Tale Reform School to avoid being seen. "She's already made me do three Magical Messages for the kingdom this week."

"Magical Messages?" I ask as three pixies fly by, shouting, "You're going the wrong way!" to anyone who will listen. The Fairy Tale Reform School kids don't seem to know about our pixie problems yet, so many turn around and dutifully head in the other direction.

Sasha's eyes flash. "Oh, you'll see." She stops in front of a classroom with a silver sign on the door that reads VILLAINS 101. "Okay, I'm off to learn the difference between true evil actions and evilness thrust upon a villain, with scroll accounts made by villains who are currently imprisoned. It's so much fun!"

"Wait! Don't leave me," I beg as Sasha slips away and traffic in the hallway begins to thin out. I'm still three corridors away from my royal seminar. I guess I could slip into this advanced wanding class or find Raina in Beauty Is Within, the class she's taking on beautification starting from the inside out. But I don't think I could survive an hour in there.

"Devin! Wait up!" Emerson cries.

I spin around, trying to squeeze between two FTRS students talking about what they were sentenced for: stealing candy and hexing a classmate they didn't like.

"Watch it," a boy says gruffly.

I see an open door to a cleaning closet and slip inside. The mirror inside it roars to life.

"Hi! This is Heathcliff White with an important Magical Message."

I hear the voice in the mirror, and I do a double take.

"A lover of the outdoors, I have always wanted to climb Mount Storybook, the highest peak in Enchantasia, and was prepared to do it on school break. But then the Battle of Rumpelstiltskin happened and our kingdom was changed forever. But that doesn't mean I can't keep doing the things I love. Our kingdom is protected by the royal guard and the finest Dwarf Police Squad in the realms. It's safe to travel again, and I can't wait to start climbing! So join me on a royal expedition the second Saturday of the month as I lead our citizens on a hike over the Troll Bridge and into Gumdrop Forest. To sign up, contact Emerson Emet at Royal Academy!"

The mirror goes dark.

Since when does Milo or Miri let anyone take over their mirrors? Heath is leading people on expeditions? And making Magical Messages like Sasha is?

Pop!

Emerson slips into the open doorway and becomes full-size, making it almost impossible for the two of us to stand in the broom closet without hitting a self-mopping mop. "Oh good, Devin, I found you! Did you hear Heath's message? He sounded so strong and confident! The perfect prince to lead us on an outdoor adventure."

"But is it even safe to be hiking with Olivina still on the loose?" I wonder aloud.

Emerson scoffs. "That woman is long gone. I'm sure of it. And more gargoyles are being rounded up each day. Plus, we're sending some royal guards to keep watch over things. It's perfectly safe and good for our citizens to see us outside again. We can't hide from villains forever." She shifts the papers in her arms and smiles. "Which is where you come in. Can you give a speech tonight? Just a teensy one?"

"A speech?" I blanch. "About what?"

"We're bringing in some of the parents from both schools to show how well our students are doing in a joint environment. If we can prove to everyone you all can get along, we can move forward post-battle." She makes a face. "You have no idea how many problems we've had throughout the countryside with citizens accusing each other of villainy or worrying their neighbors are evil. After Rumpelstiltskin, no one trusts anyone anymore! We have that Gilly Cobbler girl set to accept a Magical Medal of Honor alongside her friends for stopping the battle, and we're hoping this puts the fear out there to rest, but she's a FTRS student." Emerson sniffs. "I feel the people would respond better to someone with a royal touch telling them it's safe to get out again."

"But how do I know it's safe?" I argue. "You guys won't let us go anywhere."

"We let you go to FTRS! Sasha did her message at the *HEAS* headquarters, and Raina is leading a beauty seminar at this shop in the village called Combing the Sea. Heath is doing his hike, and Logan is going to be a guest chef at the

Three Little Pigs. We want to show people our royals are out and about and the kingdom is safe once more."

"Then why not have the royal court make appearances?" I hear the tinkling of bells and know I'm late to class. "Why would the people want to hear from kids rather than our reigning princesses?"

"Oh, we can't let them go just anywhere right now!" Emerson says with a laugh. "There is still a villain on the loose." I look at her. "Besides, they are hunkered down, busy working on putting the kingdom back together. That's why they've tapped our finest children to make speeches in their absence. You're a calming presence... You've already faced a villain and won! So what do you say? Can you speak tonight? We're having the gathering in the Rose Garden on the school grounds. Seems best not to let anyone inside again yet after what happened during the battle."

"Tonight?" I slip out the door before Emerson can stop me. "But I was going to work on a project I have for the magical creature care class I'm taking." Which is true. I was assigned to try to speak to a turtle, which means I have to go to the fountain in the Royal Underground to talk to one and then write out our whole conversation for class. Why a turtle,

I don't know. Anna gets to talk to a giraffe and is allowed to go to the FTRS class to speak to one. A giraffe! I've always wanted to talk to one of those.

"I can write you a note to do it another time," Emerson says, following me out the door. "This is more important. I'm sure your teacher will see that. Unless…would you rather we discuss that scroll course you were going to teach?" I blush and can't think of a response. "I thought so. I'll send over a gown—I haven't seen you wear anything suitable for a royal gathering since I met you—and a script. Follow that and you'll be good to go. See you in two hours!"

"Two hours? But I have class!"

With another *pop!*, Emerson disappears.

"You're going to be fine, miss…I mean, *Devin*," Brynn tells me, correcting herself yet again on not calling me *miss*. "Let's go over what you're going to say one more time."

We're in our dorm room, which is empty for once since everyone is either still in class or working on Magical Messages. Prue left a note on the magic chalkboard that says she's working the security system again in anticipation of tonight's event in the Rose Garden, and Tara scrawled a message that she's got a meeting with Headmaster Pierce. So it's just me and Brynn. I'm not sure what I'd do without my former lady-in-waiting right now. She's way better at this royal mumbo-jumbo stuff than I am.

"You're going to start by saying how delighted you are to have been asked to speak to this group tonight. Just looking out at all the parents from different school backgrounds warms your heart. Who would have ever thought Royal Academy and Fairy Tale Reform School parents or students would be working together side by side? A new dawn in Enchantasia is upon us, and you're thrilled to be a part of the changes."

"How am I a part of the changes? I'm a puppet," I complain as I lace myself into this silly dress Emerson insists I wear. It's got a corseted top, a blue lace overlay, and at least three layers on the skirt. I'd never wear anything like this in real life.

"I know," Brynn agrees. "But part of being royal is playing a role. Tonight you are playing the part of 'student helping keep parents calm during all the changes at school.' Seeing a girl who fought the fairy godmother and won will put them at ease. If you say their kids are safe, they'll believe it. That's why Emerson wants you out there with them tonight."

I look at Brynn, smiling brightly and looking effortless in a rose-colored dress that fits her like a glove. It *looks* like her. Just like the words she's helped me write for this speech feel way more her than me. She belongs in this world, and no matter how hard I try to play my part, I know deep down I do not belong here. I want something different. It's not necessarily good or bad. It's just different.

"I'll be with you the whole time, kind of." Brynn stretches out her hand and gives me something familiar. I place it in my ear.

"Couldn't do it without me, huh?" the little creature says.

"Hey, Kira," I tell the kobold who helped me navigate our undercover mission at *Happily Ever After Scrolls* headquarters when we were trying to print a story about Olivina and clear our names. Kobolds are small enough to fit in human ears so they make perfect translators for covert operations. "Nice to see you."

"Let's stick to the rules this time and do as you're told, okay?" Kira says. "I have a party with nymphs to go to later, so let's just do this speech and I'll be on my way."

"No argument there." I'm just thankful we thought of this—Brynn feeding me my lines through Kira No matter how many times we practiced the speech, I couldn't remember what Brynn wrote. Finally we decided to call on my kobold friend to relay the message. Prue helped set the whole thing up before she left, so now Brynn will be in a tower overlooking the Rose Garden feeding lines to Kira who will turn around and give them to me to relay to the group.

There is a knock on the door. Emerson pops her head inside.

"Oh good, you're ready!" She circles me appraisingly. "Nice. Very nice. A bit of rouge on your cheeks would go a long way, dear. And let's push those bangs out of your eyes. We don't want the parents thinking princesses are sloppy!" She laughs to herself and Brynn joins in good-naturedly.

"What's up with this fairy?" Kira grumbles. I just scowl.

"And Devin, don't make that face. You get such frown lines when you do! Smile now! Big and wide! It's showtime." Emerson leads me to the door. I give Brynn a worried look, but she flashes an assuring smile.

Emerson jabbers the whole way down the stairs and through the halls as we make our way to the Rose Garden.

"We've invited two dozen parents to tonight's event— half RA and half FTRS. Don't worry. All had background checks and are being checked at the door to make sure no one has any wands, bows and arrows, or spells on them to cause problems. One or two even have those new fancy ogre bodyguards everyone is talking about. I heard the waitlist is months long! I wanted your parents to be here, but your father is working. Pity. Would have been a wonderful op with reporters! Anyway, the Dwarf Police Squad is on hand to make sure nothing happens. They've got squad members at all entrances, and the courtyard is the perfect location as no one can get in or out without permission! We've never been safer!" She deposits me out the door into the garden.

I can smell the roses immediately. Rosebushes of every color line all four walls of the garden, some crawling up as high as the turret Brynn will be sitting in above it. Next to trellises and pergolas covered with pink, yellow, white, red, and even orange roses are seated two dozen sets of human, fairy, ogre, goblin, and troll parents. I have to admit, seeing them all together is a nice sight.

What isn't as pleasing is the sight of the girl shaking hands with all the parents. She's wearing a rose-colored gown that has such a large skirt she can barely fit through the aisle. Her blond hair is held in place with a tiara, and I keep hearing her say how "lovely" it is to meet everyone.

"What is she doing here?" I ask.

"Oh, yes, did I forget to mention Clarissa Hartwith is speaking with you tonight?" Emerson asks. "Such an upstanding young lady. She wanted to speak on behalf of RA. I said you already were, so she said she'd chime in. She already has a speech and everything."

I turn to Emerson in alarm. "She hates FTRS. You know that, right? She's desperate for Olivina to return and make things at RA the way they once were. Have you heard her speech yet? She's not who you want speaking."

"Oh, Devin! Don't be ridiculous!" Emerson says with a laugh. "Why would a princess bash a sister school?" She shakes her head. "Now stay right here and say hello to Clarissa, and I'll have you called on in two minutes! First, we have to play the message from Princess Snow. I just need to cue up the mirror in the garden."

Emerson pushes me out into the crowd, and Clarissa and I make eye contact and both turn away. I make myself busy checking out the layout for the event. There is a buffet of appetizers and a mirror covered with roses on the wall behind the small stage where I'll be speaking. A harp is magically playing soft music in the corner and most of the parents are quietly talking among themselves, while the Dwarf Police Squad patrols the area and *HEAS* reporters take notes. I notice right away parents are wearing either a blue FTRS pin or a gold and purple RA one.

"Hey, blondie."

"What are you doing here?" I ask as Heath steps out of the shadows holding a plate piled high with cookies, brownies, and cheese.

"They wanted a smooth-talking, adorable prince to stand alongside a princess while she spoke tonight, and of course Emerson picked me." He chomps on a cookie, getting crumbs all over the white double-breasted jacket he's wearing with navy crops and brown boots. He's also wearing the new RA/FTRS sash, which I completely forgot about. I wonder if I should have Emerson go get it to complete my "perfect princess look."

"Of course, they picked you," I agree, trying hard not to laugh. "You are perfect."

"Don't I know it? Have you heard my Magical Message?

We've got over three dozen people signed up for my hike already. Mostly girls, but still, we're going to have to open up a second hike at this point." He grins. "Emerson is loving me."

"Me, not so much," I say with a sigh. "I hate this stuff, plus I have homework with Princess Dragonfly to do."

"How is she?" he asks as he tucks into a brownie. "I hear people love her."

"I guess." I sniff. *She doesn't love me.* "I really wanted to wow her with my first assignment, but now Emerson has me doing this so I'm going to be late with it."

"I'm sure Emerson will give you a pass," Heath says. "Royal duties come first!"

I wince. That's what I hate. I just want to do work in the one class I like. But before I can say that to Heath, Clarissa's slim, pale hand appears on his shoulder.

"Heathcliff!" she says with glee. "I should have known they'd put us together for this. We do make a stunning pair."

Heath starts to choke on his brownie.

"Clarissa, can you try not to kill the prince before our address?" I pat him on the back while Clarissa glares at me.

"I'm not sure why Emerson wanted you here." She sniffs. "Maybe as a 'Royal Don't.' Or a 'Royal Killer' seeing as how you did away with Olivina. How is your traitorous friend Tara, by the way? Oh, and your new roommate, Anna Cobbler? Interesting company you're keeping, Devin."

"I could say the same of you. I saw you introducing Tara to Princess Dragonfly at the Charmed to Meet You event." For a moment, I think I see her face color, but if it does, she quickly recovers.

"Just trying to be a good Royal Academy student and make introductions. Princess Rule 78, after all," Clarissa says. "But whenever you're around Tara or Anna, things seem to go horribly wrong."

My face hardens.

Clarissa grins. "Interesting when you consider the only ones who actually claim to have dirt on Olivina are in your crew, and I can't say you're exactly trustworthy."

"I'll try not to be offended by that," Heath says, munching on another cookie.

"Oh, we're trustworthy," I counter. "All that's left to do is get rid of girls like you, and RA will be perfect."

She turns on her heels and storms away.

I grin at Heath. "You're right. Royal duties *do* come first. That was fun."

The mirror behind us roars to life and Headmistress Snow appears. "Good evening! I'm sorry I can't be with you on this momentous occasion to greet you all. I'm hard at work with Headmistress Flora of FTRS to ensure not only your students' safety, but also their livelihood during this difficult transition. I know many of you have questions, and our students will do our best to answer them for you tonight. Anything else…"

"Wait. Emerson didn't say anything about questions!" I exclaim.

"Oh boy, this should be fun," Kira whispers in my ear. "Brynn says remain calm and don't look so worried. She's scared just watching you. Project calm!"

"How can I project calm when I don't know the answers to these questions?" I hiss.

"Who are you talking to?" Heath asks, amused.

"I've got Kira with me," I admit, pointing to my ear. "And neither of us knew about these questions."

"We'll wing it," Heath says, looking unaffected as he eats a piece of cheese. "Just relax."

But I can't relax. As Snow finishes her statement, and the parents turn all eyes (some singular in the case of two troll families) on us, I am getting worked up.

"And now, may I present my brother, Heathcliff White, and fellow students Devin Nile and Clarissa Hartwith to talk to you all about this school year!" Snow finishes.

And we're on. Clarissa pushes ahead of me to stand beside Heath onstage.

"Good afternoon," Heath starts.

"*Psst!*" Kira is in my ear already. "Brynn says you're clenching your jaw and look worried. She says to relax. Your speech is flawless!"

That's because it's Brynn's speech, I want to say. I wish she was delivering it.

"We're thrilled my sister chose Devin Nile and, um, Clarissa Hartwith and myself to speak on her behalf this afternoon." Heath sounds completely at ease. He's got a natural charming smile and is making eye contact with every parent in attendance. No one can take their eyes off him (including Clarissa). Meanwhile I find I'm suddenly very itchy. I have an overwhelming desire to scratch my arm, but I know it will leave a red mark.

"Stop fidgeting!" Kira snaps. "You're giving me motion sickness."

"As students at RA who have seen their own share of

adversity, we can assure you, there is no place we'd rather be right now than here. Isn't that right, Devin?"

"Yes, I…" I wait for Kira to start speaking and feed me my lines. Kira is quiet. I tug on my ear. "I…"

"I'm waiting for Brynn," the kobold hisses. "Brynn? Come in, Brynn! There's no answer."

I smile brightly at the group. Just the sight of them in front of me is causing me to panic.

Clarissa steps in front of me. "I can answer that, Heathcliff. As a member of the Hartwith family and a fourth-generation RA student, I can say that our family has a long history with this school. It has changed of late, but I'm sure we can rise to the challenges our kingdom is facing and come out even stronger as royals always do. Don't you agree, Devin?" She smirks at me.

"Yes, well, I…am a student here," I agree, floundering. "And I feel safe! We all are. In fact, tonight, the Dwarf Police Squad is making sure no one gets in or out without permission and, um…" This isn't what I was supposed to say at all. Clarissa looks thrilled.

"Sound surer of yourself," Kira says. "I still can't reach Brynn. Brynn? Wait a minute…"

"They've protected the school before, and you've had numerous break-ins!" shouts one human dad. "What's different now?"

An ogre woman waves her hand. "How do we know our children will be protected as well as the royal students?"

"Well, royal students have always been the priority," Clarissa says, and Heath shoots her a look.

"Every student here will be treated equally, right, Devin?" Heath nudges me, but I can't stop wondering what's going on with Brynn. Where is she?

Emerson is motioning to me from the side of the garden. She makes a gesture for me to smile.

"Should we trust the FTRS kids in this castle with a villain on the loose?" a human father asks.

"Oh, so you're saying because our kids are at FTRS, they're the ones helping the villains?" asks an ogre dad. "Your royal guard let them get away the first time!"

"Brynn! Devin, something is wrong," Kira says frantically, and I hold my ear. "There's a lot of commotion and I hear Brynn yelling. Wait. What's that screeching? Oh my fairies. It's the gargoyles! They're here! Brynn! Brynn! Are you okay?"

I grab Heath's arm as my heart starts to pound.

"Devin?" Heath looks alarmed. Clarissa stares at me curiously.

"Gargoyles," I whisper.

Clarissa laughs. "Oh please, Devin. The gargoyles have all been captured."

We hear a shriek and look up as gargoyles drop into the Rose Garden.

THE DANGER WITHIN

R un!" a troll parent shouts.

People dive in every direction as a half-dozen gargoyles begin knocking over chairs and squealing as they tear the Rose Garden apart.

Clarissa screams at the top of her lungs. "Traitors! It's the FTRS students! They must have been hiding them!" She reaches for Heath's hand, but he pulls away and she races for a double window.

"They're locked!" I shout as she actually opens the windows into the castle and pulls herself through, then locks them behind her. Wait a minute. How did she know that set of windows was unlocked?

But before I can even wonder where the rest of these

gargoyles are coming from, I hear the mirror behind us fire up and start to sound the alarm. "Danger! Danger!" says the Royal Academy Security 3000 system. I watch in horror as people race for the garden door while a gargoyle tears after them, cracking two chairs in half on his way there.

"Duck!" I cry as a piece of chair comes flying toward us. Heath and I narrowly miss getting hit. I pick up the chair leg and use it to swat at the gargoyles trying to land near us. Heath grabs the back of a broken chair and does the same.

"Follow me!" Emerson instructs the parents running for their lives, trying to remain calm but failing. "All is fine. Come along now! We'll be safe in here." She tries to open the door, but it won't budge. Her wings begin to flutter extra fast. "It's locked!"

"Let me see!" says a Dwarf Police Squad member, nudging her out of the way as the rest of his crew focuses on catching the gargoyles. The dwarf tries turning the handle to no avail and then attempts kicking the door in. "Won't open! Anyone have a wand or a blaster we can hit it with? No? Maybe Lou does." He gestures toward another dwarf. "Lou? *Nooo!*"

Before anyone can respond, a gargoyle grabs Lou and hoists him into the air. A woman near me screams as he's pulled into the sky.

Pluck! Pluck! Pluck! Two more dwarves are taken away and there is a stampede to the door. People are screaming and crying. Heath and I look at each other. We can't just stand here batting gargoyles.

"You thinking what I'm thinking?" Heath asks as he knocks another gargoyle away.

"I hope so!" I pick up the hem of this annoying dress and jump off the platform. "Hang on, Kira," I shout as I dive over the overturned appetizer spread and race for the nearest Dwarf Police Squad member. I reach for the sword at his waist and pull it out of the sheath.

"*Hey!*"

"Just borrowing it!" I cry as I run back into the wide-open area. I begin swiping at the air as two gargoyles come running, looking like they want to eat me. This crew is not innocent. They're not good. *Just look at them!* I want to tell Anna. *They're evil!* At the sight of my sword, they jump back for a moment, then lunge at me again. An extra-large one with fang-like teeth darts toward me. I dive left and think I'm in the clear, then I hear a scream. I turn around. The gargoyle has grabbed an FTRS mother and is lifting her into the air.

"Help!" she cries. "Please!"

I look around for something—anything—to throw.

Ping! Something flies through the air past me. I turn around. Heath has a bag of purple things that he's throwing at the gargoyles. Is that a radish?

"An ogre family had them! The FTRS parents came prepared!" he shouts as he runs around the garden tossing radishes at the gargoyles still on the ground.

"Throw me one! Quick!" I cry.

Heath tosses me a radish, and I turn around and hurl it into the air. It hits the gargoyle in the chest. Its eyes widen in surprise, then I see them close and the gargoyle and the woman start falling to the ground at warp speed. I look around wildly for something to brace her fall and see the hammock in the corner of the garden. I yank it over just in time and she falls directly into it. *Score!* The gargoyle crashes to the ground and falls fast asleep. The others that Heath hit are already snoring. I hear a loud thump. Somebody has finally gotten the door open just as the Royal Academy Security 3000 system begins to sound inside the castle—a bit too late, frankly.

"Attack! We are under attack! Students back to their rooms immediately!"

"Brynn? Oh thank goodness!" Kira is back in my ear. "I have Brynn. She's okay. Oh, don't cry. It's okay. She's safe, but what? You saw the gargoyles coming down the hallway? They came from inside the castle?"

"How?" I wonder as we make our way indoors. "All the doors and windows in the castle have been magically locked. I have to go find Brynn," I tell Heath as the royal guard and more dwarf squad members go racing by us out to the garden to round up the gargoyles.

I run toward the tower and race up the spiral staircase. It's empty except for several mirrors that are continuing to blare, their glass swirling with a mix of red and black. "Brynn? Brynn, where are you?" I cry.

"She's at the top of the stairs," Kira tells me, and I realize that I forgot she was still in there. "But…wait. Who is she talking to? Brynn? Brynn? What's wrong? Someone's crying. Devin, I think she's in trouble! Hurry!"

"Brynn!" I shout, racing double time up the stairs until I finally reach the landing. Two figures are standing in front of an open window at the end of the hallway. I squint to see who they are, but with the flashing lights from the security system, I can't make out who it is or even hear them till I get closer. "Brynn!" I try again, but she doesn't turn around. It's only when I'm a few feet away that I hear the sobbing.

"Devin!" she says when she sees me. "Stay back!"

I stop short, not understanding. The other person removes their cloak and turns around. "Tara?" I whisper.

Her eyes are red and her under-eye circles look terrifying. She's wearing the same pantsuit I saw her in yesterday, and her red braids are frizzy as if they haven't been rebraided in days. She's gulping down tears. "Don't...come...near...me. It...isn't...safe."

Brynn looks at me, trying to convey something with her eyes. "Tara, I told you. We can trust Devin. You can tell her what you told me."

"I don't think that's a good idea." Tara's eyes shift nervously as she glances around the hallway. "I don't even know what I'd tell her."

"Exactly what you told me," Brynn tries again, patting her on the back. "Go on now. We can't help you if you don't let us. Right, Devin?"

"I want to help you," I say as I see Lily come scurrying up the staircase behind me. "What's wrong?"

Tara lets out a sob. "It's my fault."

I feel my heart thud. Brynn looks at me again. "What is?" I whisper.

"The attack." She holds her head in her hands. "I let the gargoyles in."

"That's impossible," I say, even as I remember the gargoyles bursting out of open windows. "All the windows and doors were magically sealed today before the garden party."

Lily flicks her tongue at me. *I saw Tara do it. She's telling the truth.*

"Some were open!" Tara says. "I swear! But I don't know why I did it. I don't remember!"

Brynn and I look at each other as Tara continues to cry. I feel woozy as I put the facts together—Tara's sleepwalking, the way she can't sleep at night. Not remembering where she's been.

"I don't think I should have come back here," Tara says, wiping her nose with her sleeve. "I should have stayed in the woods. It's not safe for anyone with me here. I'm evil. Just like my grandmother."

"That's not true," I insist, but inwardly, I'm worried. "It's not your fault if you can't control what you're doing. What happened exactly?"

Tara looks at me out of the corner of her eye. "I was on my way to class when I heard this voice telling me what to do. 'Let them in,' it said. 'Help them help me.' But I never saw a soul."

My heart beats faster. "Was it your grandmother? Did you see Olivina?"

Tara shakes her head. "No. And it wasn't her voice in my head either. I can't describe it. I just heard the voice and knew I had to listen. It was like my body started walking before I could even try to fight it. And the next thing I knew, I was in this hallway opening a window and the gargoyles"—she lets out another sob—"were climbing in and racing down the hall to where Brynn was standing." She holds her head again. "And that's when I snapped out of it, but it was too late."

"It's true," Brynn supplies. "I saw Tara and tried calling to her, but it was like she was in a trance. And then the gargoyles all started coming my way and the noise…the stench." She wraps her arms around herself. "It was awful. Tara was shooing them away, but they all descended on the Rose Garden before I could even warn you. Was anyone hurt?" she asks worriedly.

"I don't think so," I say, still watching Tara. "But we're all supposed to be back in our dorm rooms. The whole castle is on lockdown, if you haven't already heard the alarm."

"I'm not going to our room," Tara says quickly. "I don't want to be around anyone. I don't want to hurt you. I think this has happened before too. I keep losing chunks of time."

The hair on my arm stands up, but I stay calm. "You can't keep running. Things will never change if you don't find a way to deal with this spell you're under. Whether it's Olivina's doing or another villain. You have to let us try to help you. We know you're not evil. You just can't solve this on your own."

"What do we do?" Brynn whispers. "We have to help her. I don't think it's safe to leave her alone."

"It's not," I agree, watching Tara quiet herself as she rocks back and forth on the floor. I can see her boots now, covered in mud even though we haven't left the school in days. She's clearly disappearing and has no clue how or why. She can't go on like this. It's not safe for her, and it's not safe for us. But what will happen to her if we turn her in?

"I'm not evil. I'm not evil. I'm not evil," I hear her whisper.

I'm not sure what to do here. If a mouse with digestion

problems showed up, I'd offer him mint and call it a day, but I've never been that good at helping people. Maybe that's the problem. In my heart, I know Tara isn't evil. Someone is playing puppet master with her, and she can't control it. But she isn't safe to hide away or ignore the problem. Is this what Anna was talking to her about? Leave it to a kid with villain tendencies to wipe other villain problems under the rug. No, Tara can't do this alone and neither can I.

I need to talk to my friends.

Lily flicks her tongue again. *I can stay with her.*

I turn back to Brynn. "Do you feel comfortable staying here with Lily and Tara? I'll go get my roommates and the boys. Prue and Corden know Tara better than anyone," I say, thinking about how the three of them only had each other when they were living in the woods. "Maybe together we can figure out what to do."

Brynn straightens her shoulders. "You can count on me. I'll keep her safe till you're back."

"Tara, stay with Brynn," I instruct her. "I'll be right back."

I run back down the spiral staircase as the alarm continues to blare. Then I hear it quiet.

"Students, this is your headmaster speaking," Pierce says.

"Please lock yourselves in your rooms and stay there till we give the all clear. Please stay calm. We will get through this together!"

A royal guard is so busy listening to the message that I sneak right past him and run all the way back to my dorm room, trying to figure out what to do. This isn't Tara's fault, but with all that's happened with Olivina and the Battle of Rumpelstiltskin, and now the gargoyle attacks, I'm not sure anyone can be impartial here. What if they think Tara is a villain and is completely to blame? But if Tara cooperates and finds Olivina, wouldn't that change everything? The fear in this kingdom would be gone. We'd go back to normal, and Father would have to make good on his promise.

These are all the thoughts competing for space in my mind as I keep running.

I reach my dorm room door and throw it wide open. "Guys!" I shout. "We have a problem. We—*Oh my fairies! What is this?*"

Wailing fills the room, sounding way louder than the alarm system.

There are a half-dozen gargoyle babies in my dorm room, all being held by one or another of my friends, who look at me in alarm. Anna's face colors.

"This isn't what it looks like," Raina says as she cuddles a light-gray baby, which surprises me even more than the fact Logan is standing next to her tickling its chin.

"They're way cuter than I thought they would be," Logan says. "And at this age, they can't even bite. I think." He sniffs the air. "I'm not even allergic!"

The one Prue is holding burps. Corden seems to be trying to keep his baby from untying the bandanna he's wearing.

I glance at Sasha who is rocking one in her arms. "You too?" I say accusingly. "You just wrote a blog post about how evil they are!"

"Yes, but that was before I met the babies," Sasha explains. The one she's holding is wearing one of her pink bows. "They actually smell pretty sweet at this age, and there is no way this thing is evil. Anna's right. They're misunderstood. At least the babies are."

"Told you so," Anna says.

"Why didn't you tell us you guys found them?" Heath is holding two in his arms that look like twins. "We wouldn't have been mad or anything. But it is kind of a problem after what just happened at the garden party."

"I didn't tell you because this is exactly what I was afraid of! These babies are going to grow into evil creatures. And

Anna promised there was only one and it would stay in the forest. We can't have them in the castle!"

"We had no choice!" Anna blurts out as she rocks Edgar in her arms. "Edgar reached out in a panic and said all these parents dropped off their babies when they heard we were taking care of them."

"Who told them that?" I demand.

"Edgar," Anna says, and the baby smiles toothy fangs at me. "He's a good friend. He shared his food and water with them, and when he found out the royal guard was hunting them, he called me. I couldn't ignore them and leave all those babies out there!"

"Wait a minute. You left the castle?" I realize. "And what do you mean, Edgar called you? He came here? He can't fly long distances yet...can he?"

Anna purses her lips. "No, he was in the forest, but I *felt* him calling to me. I can't explain it. It was like I could hear him from here. They were in trouble."

"That's impossible," I stutter, flabbergasted. "Creatures can't reach us telepathically at a distance...can they?" I'm a bit freaked out. Is that even possible? And if it is, why isn't it a skill I have?

"Edgar did," Anna insists. "He told me he was in trouble and there were more babies who needed saving. Their moms didn't want her taking them away."

"Did you say *her*?" I repeat. "Who is 'her'?"

"I have no clue who he's talking about," Anna says. "I've tried asking Edgar a few times." The baby is now chewing on a strand of Anna's hair and looking perfectly content.

Dimitri! Edgar says pointing to me and clearly mixing me up with the carrier dove. *Dimitri!*

"No, that's Devin," Anna corrects him. "The one who helped us the other day. Tell her what happened, Edgar."

Edgar looks at me, his oversize yellow eyes sad. *She took Mama. She said we're next.*

"Who, Edgar?" I ask, coming closer. The rest of my friends draw near. I see Sasha's quill fly through the air, poised to write. "Who said that?" *Olivina*, I think. *It has to be Olivina. Please be Olivina and we can be done with all this.*

The girl, Edgar says, and my blood runs cold. *The girl with the red hair.*

TOUGH CHOICES

Edgar means Tara. That's the only explanation. Which means Tara is right—she's being controlled by Olivina.

Or she's acting on her own free will and is actually evil and trying to deceive us all.

Or the gargoyles are trying to deceive us.

Maybe Edgar is the evil one and just looks vaguely cute.

How am I supposed to know what's true and what's not? If I'm wrong about Tara, then maybe I'm wrong about the gargoyles too. My head is spinning. I just don't know anymore!

"Devin? Are you okay?" Raina tries.

I can feel Anna's eyes on me. She knows what Edgar said. She has to know, if she can understand him. Now she's just waiting for me to tell the others that the girl who once saved us from a villain is still being controlled by one. And I just can't do it. How can I trade Tara for baby gargoyles I don't trust either?

"Oh man, this one has gas." Heath starts to cough as the twin gargoyles laugh. "They both have gas! Someone open a window if the security system is off again."

Logan runs over to the window and it miraculously opens. Dimitri glides right into our room.

Dimitri! Dimitri! Dimitri! Edgar squeaks happily pointing to the bird, then me, then the bird again. So clearly, we're both Dimitri.

"Has anyone seen Tara since the gargoyles attacked?" Prue's glittery face looks worried. "I'd hate to think she's out in the castle somewhere on her own."

"I'm sure she's okay," I say automatically instead of telling them the truth: Brynn is with Tara. Tara let the gargoyles in! But with Edgar and the babies here with Anna, I can't decide who to trust anymore.

Dimitri interrupts my thoughts. *Devin, I came as fast as I could. This was only the gargoyles' first attack. There is still a large gathering of gargoyles in the west end of the Hollow Woods.*

My cousin Rainy was making a nest in a tree above them and heard them say they're just waiting on the signal to attack.

Anna holds Edgar tighter and watches me closely.

Attack where? I chirp.

Dimitri blinks. *He said he heard them say 'the royal court.' Some big medal ceremony for kids who stopped Rumpelstiltskin.*

Anna and I look at one another.

"My sister," Anna whispers.

"What's going on?" Heath asks. "What are you two talking to that pigeon about?"

"He's a dove," Anna and I say at the same time.

"Attention, students," says Milo via mirror. "As many of you have heard by now, there was an incident this afternoon in the Rose Garden where a small group of gargoyles invaded the grounds."

"We understand this is scary," adds Miri, "but it's important for you to know the gargoyles that attacked have been apprehended, as have dozens of others in the Hollow Woods."

Not all of them, Dimitri chirps.

"Fairy be, hide the babies!" Raina hisses. "Before Miri and Milo see them."

Everyone quickly rushes to put the babies in Raina's hope

chest and motions for them to be quiet. Heath stands in front of the chest with Logan to block the view.

"Our royal guard won't rest till every last gargoyle is apprehended and tried for their crimes," Milo says.

All six babies in the room start to whimper.

"Shh!" Sasha says to the babies. "You'll give yourself away!"

"I've got this!" Logan opens his sack and starts handing out rolls to each baby. They take them in their chubby claws. "Fresh out of the oven. This will keep them busy for a while."

"We urge all students to speak up as we try to put this terror to bed," adds Milo.

"If anyone has any information on how the gargoyles got into Royal Academy, we urge you to come forward," Miri says.

"And if you have information about any rogue gargoyles, don't be afraid to speak up," Milo says. "Tell your teachers."

"Thank you for your help, students," Miri adds. "It is now safe to roam around the castle once more."

We all look at one another.

"What are we going to do?" Logan gulps. "If Miri and Milo find out any of them are in here—"

"She won't," Anna interrupts. "We'll keep them quiet and hidden till we can figure out what to do."

"What *are* we going to do?" Heath asks. "Keep them? Hide them from their parents? Deprogram them so they don't grow up and become villains?"

My thoughts exactly.

Raina frowns. "My brother has a point. We don't know what we're dealing with here. They're cute and all, but can we trust them?"

"They're not villains!" Anna insists. "Their parents have been brainwashed by—" She looks at me. "Are you going to tell them the truth, or am I?"

"What's going on?" Heath sounds wary.

"You don't know that they're telling the truth," I counter as everyone looks at me. "They didn't even have a name."

"They know what they saw," Anna insists as Edgar chews his roll and looks back and forth between us. "They know who is responsible!"

"Do they?" I jut out my chin. "What if they're lying? How can you trust them over her?"

"Guys, what's going on?" Sasha asks. "What do you know that we don't?"

Anna looks at me again. The babies look at me. My roommates and friends look at me. And I've never felt more confused. Why did I think coming here would give me clarity? "I need to get some air," I tell them, brushing past Anna.

"Wait! Devin!" Anna grabs my arm. "Where are you going? You aren't going to report the babies, are you?" Her pale face looks even paler than normal.

"I just need to think" is all I say before closing the door behind me. Back inside the room, I hear everyone talking at once.

I don't know where I'm going, but I know I have to get out of here. I rush down the hall, passing two girls—one RA and one FTRS—having a sing-off in the hallway mirrors, which Milo is currently judging. ("Too pitchy," he tells both of them. "You need practice.") I keep going, passing three girls teaching FTRS girls how to balance a book on their heads (seriously?) and an FTRS goblin girl telling three RA girls in ball gowns the easiest way to pick a lock.

"None of this gargoyle business would happen under Olivina's watch," I hear a new voice say. "Say what you want, she kept this school safe!"

Clarissa. I stop at the edge of a large potted tree in the hallway and spy Clarissa sitting by the fountain entrance to the Royal Underground. She's sitting with a group of princesses who all look like they could be clones—same dress, different colors, same jewelry, same updo, same small tiara and handheld mirror used for touching up makeup, and most of all, same look of adoration on their face when they look at Clarissa. She is their queen and they're hanging on her every word.

"Think about it. The minute Olivina was ousted, what happened next? Rumpelstiltskin attacked! Half the kingdom was destroyed! The fairy godmother could have protected us way better than the royal court did," Clarissa sniffs. "At least that's what my mother said in the scroll she sent this morning by Pegasus Post."

"But did Olivina know Rumpelstiltskin?" one girl asked. "Maybe she was working with him too."

"Never," Clarissa defends. "The fairy godmother just wants what's best for royals. I don't know about the Fairy Tale Reform School kids, but…"

"But wait. Didn't Olivina trick all the royals into thinking they needed her help as a fairy godmother to survive their fairy tales?" asks a girl with brown hair. "I thought she played them all."

"I mean, maybe," Clarissa says as she applies lip gloss. "But is that so wrong? Look how famous she's made the royal court! Every one of those princesses are rulers now thanks to her. She taught them how to survive. Sometimes you have to bend people to your will to make them see reason. If it's for the greater good, then it's all worth it in the end."

Anger bubbles up inside me and I can't help myself. "Is that why you let the gargoyles in this afternoon at the tea party?" I ask, striding toward her so quickly, Clarissa backs up and practically lands in the fountain. "How did you know one of the windows in the Rose Garden was unlocked? You were the only one able to escape the gargoyles this afternoon. My guess? Maybe you *knew* what was going to happen."

Her friends gasp. One turns to her and says, "Clarissa, that's not true, is it?"

"Of course not!" Clarissa rolls her eyes. "I was just trying to get away from those beasties like everyone else. It's not like I let them in to destroy the ceremony."

My ears perk up. "How did you know someone let them in?"

Clarissa pales. "What?"

"I said, how did you know someone let them in?"

"I…I'm just assuming," Clarissa backpedals. "I could see someone like Tara doing something like that."

I smile wickedly. "Funny you should mention Tara. So tell me again, how did you know that one window was open?"

Clarissa sighs. "I told you! I tried a window, and it happened to be open. I locked it again because I was trying to prevent them from getting in." She holds her chin high. "I was protecting my castle."

I growl. "You were protecting yourself!" I pull her away from the others and whisper in her ear. "First, you accuse Tara of being the real villain problem in this school. Then, I catch you introducing her to Princess Dragonfly at Charmed to Meet You. Feels suspicious."

Clarissa pushes a loose strand of curls behind her right ear. "Tara," she sputters. "You were clearly seeing things. Why would I talk to Tara after how she turned on Olivina and lied about her own grandmother?"

"I don't know. But when our teachers hear what happened today, and Tara gives her side of the story, I suspect they'll want to know what you were talking to her about when you supposedly dislike her so much."

Clarissa looks mildly concerned. I continue. "And if they

find out you did something to Tara… Well, let's just say get ready for some detention at Fairy Tale Reform School."

Her face reddens. "Like my parents would ever let me set foot at that school. Why, I'd move to another kingdom before I'd stay in one that would consider letting someone like Brynn Haun be in charge."

I flash a devilish smile. "Well, maybe you'll get your wish. I'd start packing." I start walking.

"Devin?" Clarissa's voice squeaks. "Devin? Where are you going? *Devin!*"

I keep walking and don't look back.

CHAPTER 16

CHOICES

I know where I'm headed now. I go straight to the secret entrance to Headmistress Snow's office. I'm hoping Snow or Headmaster Pierce is in there so I can talk to them. They'll know what to do about everything. I'm sure of it.

Seeing the headmaster's elevator next to the gurgling fountain gives me flashbacks of the day we tried to sneak into Olivina's office, but I push the thoughts aside and head up. The door to the office is already open and I can see the lights flickering inside, so someone must be here. I take a deep breath and push the door open wider. Someone is sitting at the large gold-leafed desk, their back to me. I see Snow's dark hair and perk up.

"Headmistress Snow? It's Devin Nile." The desk chair starts

to spin around. "I need to talk to—oh, Princess Dragonfly." I start backing away. "Sorry to bother you."

"Hello, Devin," she says pleasantly. "Can I help you with something?"

"Sorry, I was looking for Headmistress Snow." I may have told Clarissa I'd call her out to a teacher, but a problem this big should really be reserved for the headmasters.

Princess Dragonfly's long face is pulled into a deep frown. "She's been called off to an emergency meeting with the royal court, I'm afraid, and she asked me to sit in for her till she returns. Unfortunately, this gargoyle incident has sent parents from both schools into a tizzy. They don't get how something like this could happen under our esteemed headmasters' watch." She rises from the chair and comes around the desk. "Is there anything I can help you with in their absence?"

I hesitate. The smell of chocolate chip cookies that radiates off her is very soothing, but I try to resist. Princess Dragonfly doesn't know Tara. What if she rushes to judgment? "It's okay. It can wait. Thanks!" I turn to leave.

"I was just grading your first paper, by the way."

I turn and look at her. She's leaning back on the desk,

her long, green dress billowing out, looking much like the netting on her wings when she's in dragonfly form.

"Do you want to know your grade? I know you've been busy with your other duties and you had to rush this assignment, but despite that, you still managed an A minus. It's impressive work."

"Really?" I perk up. I was sure my teacher didn't like me, and after that rush job I did on it I thought I'd failed. "You liked it?"

"I truly did. You're clearly a talented emerging creature caretaker, which is why I've been so hard on you, I'm afraid. I see a lot of me in you, and if you're going to be truly great, you need to work harder than the others in the room. You can't be mediocre."

I pull my shoulders back. "I won't be."

She smiles. "I know you won't." She cocks her head to one side. "I guess I just don't understand what you're doing here. Why aren't you at a real creature caretaker school like the one I taught at in Nottingham?"

I step back into the room again. "I love the Nottingham School for Nature and Wild Beasts," I say breathlessly. "I've read the brochure forward and backward."

"Then why don't you apply?"

My face falls. "My parents don't want me transferring right now with everything going on in the kingdom."

She makes a sort of buzzing noise with her teeth. "Pish posh! You're safer in Nottingham than you are here!"

"That's what I said!"

Princess Dragonfly picks up a gold vase sitting on the desk and moves it over a few inches. "Well, if you continue to do well in my class, I see no reason why I can't write you a recommendation to the school and speak to your parents personally. A talent like yours shouldn't be wasted here at RA, no offense."

"You'd do that?" I ask, barely able to contain my excitement. "That would be... Wow. Yes. Thank you, Princess Dragonfly!"

"Of course." She touches my hand. "But I do wish you felt comfortable enough to open up to me about whatever is bothering you. You're *sure* there is nothing I can do for you in Snow's absence? You seemed quite tense when you walked in here."

"Oh." My excitement fades. "*That*. I..."

"Devin, it's all right. Whatever you tell me stays between us and Snow and Pierce when they return."

"Professor Pierce went there too?" I ask. Why didn't Princess Dragonfly mention that earlier?

"Oh yes! Did I not mention that?"

Princess Dragonfly walks over to the couch and pats the seat next to her. "But they may not be back today or tomorrow. There is a lot to sort out with the royal court, so if this is urgent, you might want to tell me. I've got your back."

I exhale. If Snow and Pierce put her in charge, then I must be able to trust her. I sit down next to her and look into her bug-like eyes. Where to start... Do I tell her about Tara? Or the gargoyles? Both? One? "It's about the gargoyle attack," I blurt out before I can second-guess myself.

She raises her right eyebrow. "Do you know something about how they got into the school?" I hesitate. "Devin, I can't help you if you don't tell me."

"Someone helped them," I admit. "Not on purpose. I think the person was under a spell." I think of Clarissa. "I also think another student might somehow be involved, but I'm not sure how. The student is very loyal to Olivina unfortunately."

She leans forward, smelling sweet like chocolate. "Really? Well, we'll deal with that student later. But first: Who helped the gargoyles? Do you know where we can find more creatures?"

"I…" I'm sweating. I think of Edgar's sweet face. "Do you think all gargoyles are bad? Or could they be under a spell too?"

"What makes you say that?" she asks.

"I saw a baby flying with its mother the other day during the magic carpet attack," I admit. "It didn't look like it was trying to hurt us."

"Did it talk to you?" she asks curtly.

"No," I say quickly, seeing her reaction. "I just got the feeling it was innocent."

"It's not. They're very dangerous, Devin." Her face falls. "If I could tell you the things young gargoyles are capable of… I had issues with one with my daughter… Well, you wouldn't think they're innocent at all."

"I'm sorry," I say. "Is your daughter okay?"

Princess Dragonfly looks far away. "That's a long story for another day." She takes my hand in her cool one. "My point is, they may look sweet and innocent, but they quickly turn into something dark and nasty. We need to find them before they mature. If you know something…"

I hesitate.

"So there *are* gargoyles here in the castle," she guesses.

"From the look on your face, I'd suspect babies, which is good. They aren't dangerous—yet."

I feel my heart beating fast. I'm torn. I know Anna wants to protect them, but what if she can't protect herself?

"Devin, I promise you no harm will come to the babies, but we must secure them before…they do damage. You have to trust me. Where are they? Who is helping them?"

I can't seem to speak. Am I betraying Anna and Tara or helping them by telling?

Princess Dragonfly stands up. "Well, I can see I'm going to get nowhere. If you can't put your faith in me, I understand, but it does make me question your loyalties. I'm not sure I can recommend such a student to Nottingham."

My heart feels like it stops beating. No! I need Princess Dragonfly to back me up on a transfer! To convince my parents! If she doesn't, I may never get to that school. I can see it as clear as day: if I stay here, I'll be stuck living the rest of my life as a royal

"There are babies in my dorm room," I blurt out. I see her stricken face and start talking fast. "I didn't bring them there. Someone else did," I say, thinking of Anna. "But what you really need to know is about the adult gargoyles that got into the Rose Garden. Tara, Olivina's granddaughter, let them in. She doesn't even remember doing it, which is what scares me. She's been bewitched and she doesn't want to hurt anyone. She's good, I'm sure of it, but I don't want anyone else getting hurt."

Princess Dragonfly walks over to me again. "Don't worry. We can help her together! Where is Tara right now?"

"On the top floor of the girls' dormitory turrets. The lookout post." I pause, thinking again of Tara looking so scared and frightened, not understanding what's happening to her. I'm doing the right thing, I tell myself. "Are you sure you can help her?"

She squeezes my hand so tightly I wince. "Don't you worry. I'll take care of this myself so there are no screw-ups with the royal guard or the Dwarf Police Squad again. Once I have them, I'll alert the royal court and this whole villain witch hunt will finally be over."

"Should I go with you to try to explain?" I feel my stomach do flips.

"No, I think it's best if you don't come anywhere near Tara or the gargoyles. I don't want them corrupting you when you're so emotional." She smiles. "You just go find a quiet place to sit and work on that Nottingham application. I'm going to need it right away!"

Princess Dragonfly rushes out, leaving the scent of fresh-baked cookies in her wake. I pray Tara and Anna can forgive me.

SECOND GUESSES

When I step into the hallway a few moments later, Princess Dragonfly is long gone.

I glance at the mirror to my right, waiting for it to come alive and tell us all to head back to our rooms for safety. Princess Dragonfly would certainly take precautions to ensure no one sees the gargoyle babies or Tara being carted away. Where is she taking Tara anyway? Why didn't I think to ask?

I'm not sure where to go. Princess Dragonfly said to stay away from the gargoyles and Tara, but heading to the Royal Underground to write my entrance essay to Nottingham feels wrong. I feel sick when I think about how I'm possibly gaining entrance to this school. Edgar's little face flashes in my mind again, and my stomach lurches.

This is wrong.

What have I done, letting Princess Dragonfly take them away? I've made a mistake. I have to make Princess Dragonfly see reason. Maybe we can help Tara and the babies without turning them over. Running as fast I can, I sprint all the way to our dorm room. I hear crying before I even reach the open door.

"*You!*" Anna cries when she sees me. My other roommates cram around her. "You're a traitor! How could you do this to them? They're babies!"

My cheeks burn. "I was trying to do the right thing. Royals are supposed to keep law and order."

"Forget acting like a royal," Anna spits out. "You didn't even behave like a decent human being. You turned them in to save yourself. Princess Dragonfly told us the deal you made!"

My cheeks burn. Why would the princess tell my friends about Nottingham?

"Some royal you are! I have to go find them!" Anna tears off into the hallway.

"Anna! Wait!" Raina cries, but Anna keeps running.

"I can't believe you went to talk to the headmasters without talking to us first," Sasha says quietly.

I look at the others. "There was no time to talk. I was

trying to stop a villain outbreak! You didn't see Tara. Most of you didn't see what happened in the Rose Garden either. We were under attack. Someone has to stop the gargoyles and Olivina before it's too late." I look at Heath for backup, but he looks away.

"You know I usually take your side, but what we saw in the Rose Garden and what just happened with the babies is very different," he says slowly. "You can see that, right?"

"We're not mad. We're just confused," Raina adds. "You say you want to be a magical creature caretaker. Aren't they supposed to protect all animals?"

"*Good* animals," I clarify.

Raina cocks her head to the side. "What about the baby gargoyles didn't seem good to you?"

I'm quiet.

"I know I should be skeptical, but they seemed sweet," Sasha agrees. "Edgar liked you. I know you were trying to do the right thing, but my reporter's hunch tells me this is wrong."

I'm not sure what to say.

"What did Snow say when you told her about them?" Logan asks. "And why did she send Princess Dragonfly instead of coming herself?"

"I didn't see Snow," I admit, my cheeks burning again. "She and Headmaster Pierce are away the next few days for royal court business. I told Princess Dragonfly because she's in charge right now."

Heath frowns. "Why would they put a new teacher in charge instead of Headmistress Flora of FTRS? Or Princess Rose? That doesn't make sense."

"I don't know." The pit in my stomach grows. "She was in their office when I got there and said they asked her to look after things."

"In *their* office?" Heath interrupts. "Why wouldn't she just leave a note telling people to come see her in her office? My sister never lets anyone in her office when she's not there. There are too many sensitive scrolls lying around."

Now my heart is pounding. The more they talk, the more something feels off about the conversation I had with Princess Dragonfly. Have I placed *Tara* in danger by sending her off with Princess Dragonfly? "I have to go find Tara," I say.

"No one has seen her or Brynn since the lockdown," Logan says. "Corden and Prue went out to look for them."

"If Brynn hasn't come back either, maybe Princess

Dragonfly has them both. Oh no…" What if she's taken them and fled the castle?

"Dev, what is going on?" Sasha asks.

I suddenly feel ill. "I think the princess has Brynn, Tara, and the baby gargoyles and she's…."

"She's *what*?" Heath presses.

I think I might be sick. "I'm not sure if I should have trusted Princess Dragonfly," I say. "Don't ask me why I think that. I just do. I think I've made a huge mistake." I close my eyes. "I just did the most unroyal thing I ever could—turned in innocent creatures and a confused girl who needed help, just to get myself into a school," I whisper. "I need to find them before anyone else gets hurt."

"Okay," Sasha says, grabbing a cloak and not questioning my reasoning. "We'll go with you."

Relief washes over me. I've screwed up, but my friends still have my back. It only makes me feel worse about what happened with Tara.

"There's only one person who can truly help us," I say.

A girl who can hear creatures from a great distance. Unlike me. I whistle and a carrier pigeon lands on our windowsill.

Be on the lookout for a dragonfly or a woman with a girl who has red hair, I tell the pigeon. *She might be heading to Fairy Tale Reform School or the Hollow Woods or...the royal court. Find them and report back to me.*

Got it! the bird says and takes off.

I look at the others. "I have a lot to explain, I know, but trust me—we need to find Princess Dragonfly and those gargoyle babies fast."

"Devin, you're not making sense," Raina says.

"Gather all the weapons we have at our disposal— including your compact, Sasha. Find Corden and Prue, and meet me back here in fifteen minutes." I race out the door.

"Where are you going?" Logan asks.

I turn around. "I have to go find Anna Cobbler."

I don't have to go far. She's exactly where I'd expect to find a girl who just learned she can speak to animals—in the Pegasi stables trying to coax one to fly her out of here.

I know I'm wearing the wrong uniform, but we have Pegasi at my school too, I hear Anna say as she pets one of the white Pegasi's manes. *My sister has been a great friend to Pegasi over the years, and I'm prepared to become one. I just need a lift to the Hollow Woods. Or rather over the woods.*

"They're not going to listen to you," I say and she looks up. "They're royal Pegasi."

Her face changes. "Go away, traitor. I can convince them to help me on my own. I need to go save Edgar."

I step in front of her. "I know. That's why I'm here. To help you."

"*You?* Help *me*? You just turned the gargoyles in!" Anna moves through the stalls, and I follow her.

Fight! Fight! Fight! I hear the Pegasi say as they peek out of their stalls to see what's going on.

"I made a mistake," I say, apologizing. "And not just with the gargoyles. With Tara too." Anna's eyes narrow. "I think I trusted the wrong person, Princess Dragonfly, who...I think...is working for Olivina." Anna's eyes widen. "Maybe! I'm not sure! I don't know anything anymore!" I sit down on a bale of hay. "I've made quite a mess of things."

"Oh, you're just realizing that now? Thanks to you, our chance to find out who is controlling the gargoyles is gone and so is Tara." Anna says, her face filled with fury. She's at least two inches shorter and yet she looks like she could take me down.

"I know," I say. "That's why I'm here. We can team up

and find them." Anna snorts. "I'm serious. We both care about animals."

"*I* care about *all* animals," she counters. "There's a difference."

Burn! one of the Pegasi comments.

I look at the hay on the floor and hear the soft neighing of the horses in nearby stalls, all moving around restlessly, hating that we've brought our argument to them when all they want is peace. "You're right," I say softly, petting the nose of a Pegasus named Charlie. "I've been so caught up in figuring out how to be the most epic magical creature caretaker in the kingdom that I forgot how to care about creatures that are different from the ones I know, like gargoyles." Anna looks at me. "I thought if I could hear Edgar, it meant *I* was evil so I was afraid."

"I knew it!" Anna says triumphantly.

"But I didn't realize I was ignoring Edgar's cry for help. I've always been told gargoyles are bad, so I believed it, instead of getting to know Edgar and the gargoyles and listening to what they have to say." I swallow hard. "I guess I'm not such a good caretaker after all." Anna doesn't contradict me. "I know I can't make up for how I behaved, but I do want to try to help Edgar now. It took me a while to realize all this, but now

I think I know how to find the person bewitching the remaining gargoyles and stop her, but I need your help." I pause.

Anna looks at me. "This sounds like a rogue-royal move." Her mouth twitches. "If you're wrong, it might get you sent to my neck of the woods."

I think of serving a sentence at Fairy Tale Reform School. It's not my first choice, but if that's what happens… "It's a risk I'm willing to take," I say firmly. "I can't sit back and do nothing. Besides, I've never fit in here anyway."

Anna is quiet for a moment, and I hear a tail swishing in a nearby stall. "I know what you mean." She steps closer to me. "I've always lived in my sister's shadow. Always been compared to her. And now that she's the hero in our fairy tale, I always will be the runner-up. It's hard to fit in when you were born to stand out."

"Yes." Maybe we understand each other better than I thought. "I can't do this on my own. I need someone who can hear creatures from a great distance to help me track down Tara, Princess Dragonfly, Edgar, and possibly even Olivina. Will you help me?"

Anna offers me her hand, and yanks me up. "I was wondering when you'd finally ask."

How to Catch a
Fairy Godmother

So maybe fifteen minutes was a bit ambitious, but in less than an hour we're all assembled back in the Pegasi stables and Anna and I are briefing the group on all the ways I've screwed up today. I can't believe they're still talking to me after what I've done.

"Princess Rule 19: The finest princesses learn from their mistakes," Raina says diplomatically.

"Princess Rule 20: And make up for their lapses in judgment with action," Sasha adds and Raina does a double take. "I may not like the Royal Academy Rules, but that doesn't mean I haven't memorized them!"

"So let's get out of here and fix this," Logan agrees. "I'm worried about Brynn. No one's been able to reach her by mini magical scroll. Wherever Princess Dragonfly has gone, she's taken Brynn with her."

"Because Princess Dragonfly is working with Olivina," I say, thinking again of the conversation I had with Clarissa. "She has to be."

"So what are we still doing here?" Heath asks. "Let's find them before Princess Dragonfly, Olivina, or any of the gargoyles she's possessed attack the school. Enchantasia can't handle another battle."

"I just need a few more minutes to deactivate the security system." Prue punches at her security scroll. "Since the whole castle is still on lockdown, the system will set off an alert the minute we try to leave the grounds, but if I do this…" I hear a beep. "We have fifteen minutes to get out of here," she says triumphantly.

I motion to the Pegasi. "Then let's go!"

"I think a few of us should stay back here to give you time," Corden says. "Teachers are going to come looking for you when you disappear. You need a cover."

"Especially you," Prue says, pointing to Anna. She punches at her scroll again. "I can stall the security system for an additional fifteen minutes, but after that, the royal guard will come after you. We can help you more if we're here on the ground."

"Thanks, guys," I say gratefully. "Then let's get out of here before anyone comes looking." I go to the nearest stall and open it. Charlie the Pegasus pops out.

Hi there, I say in clicks. *We're going to go rescue some friends and we need your help.*

That's what I'm here for! The white horse flaps his majestic silver wings and steps out of the stall. *Where are we headed?*

That's what we need to figure out! I turn to Anna. "You're on."

Anna shifts uncomfortably. "This isn't going to work."

"It is," I insist. "You were able to contact Edgar last time even though he was way across the Hollow Woods and nowhere near RA! You can reach him now."

"But the first time I did it, Edgar contacted *me*," Anna says worriedly. "I didn't do anything. I just listened."

"Well, this time you're going to do the talking," I tell her. "Look, I know this creature caretaker stuff is all new to you, but you have a gift that's way stronger than mine." I try not to feel a tweak envious. "Let me help you learn how to use it. Close your eyes," I say softly. "Imagine connecting with an animal you don't know how to speak with. That's how I first started to speak bear actually. It was a mistake."

"No way," Anna says as she closes her eyes.

"Way! Now call to Edgar and see if you can hear him."

"Out loud?"

"Umm…" I have no idea how this animal telepathy works, but it can't hurt. "Try it both ways—in your head and out loud."

Anna takes a deep breath and emits a high-pitched squeaking noise that sounds a lot like the gargoyles. Charlie the Pegasus grows restless so I pat his side. Anna pauses for a moment, then tries again as the rest of us watch. I can sort of make out what she's saying: *Edgar, want to help. Where are you?*

Anna gasps. "I hear him!" She jumps up and down. "I can hear him!" Her eyes are bright. "He says they're in a tower. A watchtower? On a hill?"

The rest of us look at one another. Where is that?

"Got it," Prue says, punching at her scroll again. "He must mean 'Fort Enchantasia, which was once intended to be the home of the royal guard and was abandoned before completion due to a disagreement over location and lack of space,'" she reads from her scroll. "'A new fort was built at Camp Humpty Dumpty, leaving the incomplete Fort Enchantasia abandoned. Its watchtower is now a popular hiking spot for villagers.'"

"Huh. Wonder why I've never been," Heath murmurs as he saddles up a Pegasus.

"It's popular with hikers because it has terrific views of the kingdom and overlooks"—Prue looks at us—"Royal Court Manor."

"Where the royal court is assembled today to give out the Magical Medal of Honor to my sister and her friends," Anna realizes. "What if Princess Dragonfly is going to ambush them?"

"She won't!" Corden insists. "We'll stop her!"

The rest of us are high-fiving when suddenly we hear Anna cry out.

"No, Edgar! Don't listen to her. We're coming! We're coming!" Anna says before squeaking the same message. "She's getting ready to send them out into battle," she tells me. "He says she's trying to force even the babies to fight. He says…" She scrunches her eyes tight again. "He says…bring strawberries?" She opens her eyes. "Why do we need strawberries?"

"I don't know." I'm stumped. "I've never used strawberries

for healing before." I turn to Charlie. *Do you know what strawberries are for?*

Charlie's tail swishes. *Not a clue! I have never had one before.*

Lily flicks her tongue. *Radishes and strawberries have been missing from crops for a while now due to Rumpelstiltskin and the gargoyles.*

"Radishes put gargoyles to sleep, but what do strawberries do?" Sasha mounts a Pegasus named Seymour. "They must do something, right? Why else would he want you to bring them?"

"Hang on!" Logan runs out of the stables and comes back a few moments later. He's carrying something in the front of his shirt, which he's turned into a makeshift basket. "From my vegetable garden. We haven't been able to grow any in a while, but post-battle I tried again and look! These are my first strawberries." He dumps them out on a table in the stables. I watch the perfectly ripe fruit roll across the wood.

I pick one up and smell it. "I haven't seen actual strawberries in forever."

Charlie bites at the air, trying to grab the piece of fruit. *Smells good!*

Logan snatches the strawberry back. "We need these. I had to add some spells to make them grow faster, but at least we have a few dozen." He grabs a sack off one of the pegs on the wall and puts the strawberries inside it. "I'll hang on to them for safekeeping."

The mirror in the stable starts to blare. "Security breach! Security breach! Students spotted leaving grounds!"

"That's you, guys," Prue says. "I can't turn off Miri as well as I can Milo. She must have heard your plan."

"Go! We'll hold the other teachers off," Corden adds, grabbing a broom from the corner of the room and brandishing it like a weapon.

I'm not sure that's going to do much, but I don't argue. I pull myself up onto Charlie, and Logan, Heath, Sasha, Raina, and Anna do the same with their own Pegasi. Heath gallops toward the stable doors and throws them open when he gets near. The alarm blares louder.

"Professor Harlow isn't the easiest to hold back," Anna warns.

"Let us worry about her," Prue says. "You guys get out of here!"

I start to gallop, picking up speed as I follow the others. I can hear commotion behind me as I reach the doors. Charlie, free of confinement, can finally expand his massive wings. He does a long stretch and then takes to the air just as I see a few teachers running out of the stables behind us. I look back.

"Anna, get back here!" I hear Headmistress Flora shout.

But we're already gaining altitude and flying toward the sun.

CHAPTER 19

MOMENT OF TRUTH

Flying a Pegasus is a lot more enjoyable than riding in a carriage. Or on a magic carpet. In fact, I think I should do all my traveling by Pegasus now. Not only is Charlie a smooth flier, but he's also a great confidant. The others are flying ahead of us so Charlie and I are all alone up here. I wind up pouring my heart out to him as we fly over Fairy Tale Reform School and head toward the village. The Royal Court Manor is on the other side of it, which means Fort Enchantasia is there too, and there's plenty of time to talk.

Look, don't beat yourself up for wanting to try something new, Charlie tells me. *Nottingham is a great place. I've been there and I think you'd like it. When something doesn't feel right, you just know.*

It's true, I agree. *I'm just not sure I deserve a fresh start.*

Of course you do! We all do! Listen, a lot of people don't know this about me, but before I came to work at Royal Academy, my first job was at the Enchantasia Village stables shepherding shoppers all over the kingdom. While I liked the different views, I felt like I was always being told what to do, where to go, what time to leave. I wanted to be in more control. So I applied for a transfer to Royal Academy, and I've never been happier.

I smile and pat Charlie's mane. *I'm happy for you, but I don't know if I deserve a fresh start after what I've done. I'm not sure if I'm a strong enough magical creature caretaker to get into Nottingham anyway.*

What do you mean? Charlie snorts in aggravation. *You're a great creature caretaker! Not many people can speak Pegasus, or get Pegasi to agree to help them. I heard all about what you did that day in the village a few months back when you and your friends needed to hitch a ride. Those Pegasi wouldn't have helped you if they didn't think they could trust you. Trust is very important when it comes to animals.*

I think of Edgar and wince. I completely betrayed his trust. Same with Anna. I eye her ahead of me, her teal skirt flapping in the wind, revealing her striped tights. *I've let down those that trusted me—Tara, Edgar, my friends, I tell Charlie. I don't know if what I did is forgivable.*

Of course it is! You're doing the right thing now! And that's what's important! Look! Charlie turns his nose in the direction he wants to fly and we make a hard right, flying over teacup and large boot homes in the village. *There's Fort Enchantasia straight ahead!*

High on a hill, I see the watchtower alongside a half-built wall and several crumbling structures. I pull back my shoulders and stare straight ahead. Charlie is right. I can fix this. I just have to use my instincts to make the right decisions. The area looks deserted, but looks can be deceiving. Beyond the tower, I see the flags of the Royal Court Manor in the distance. Below the fort is a ridge that looks like a hiking trail. While the watchtower is closest, my gut tells me we should avoid landing in such an open area.

Probably best we don't land in the fort, I tell Charlie. Can you tell the others to land on the trail below it?

You got it! Charlie says, and I hear him radio the other Pegasi. Within minutes we land on the dirt path. Anna comes running up to me. Her face is tearstained.

"Edgar was trying to reach me the whole flight," Anna says. "What if we're too late? He kept saying, 'Hurry. She's coming back.'"

I frown and look up at the wall to see if anyone is on lookout. I still don't see Princess Dragonfly. "I wonder why she would have left the babies and flown off."

"I don't know. He said something about her coming back to send them to the attack. He definitely means they're headed to the royal court to disrupt the medal ceremony my sister is at." Anna frowns. "He also said she took the girl with red hair with her." Anna starts to squeak again and then closes her eyes and listens. "The babies are alone right now. We have to get up there."

"Wait! We can't be rash. We need a plan."

"Devin is right," Heath says. "If Princess Dragonfly has Tara and she brought her here, my guess is she's probably going to try to control Tara and use her to attack the royal court." Heath's face is grim.

"This all adds up," I say, looking at the others. "Tara has been complaining she hasn't been sleeping well, and Lily saw her sleepwalking, which Tara never remembered. If Princess Dragonfly—and Clarissa—have been using Tara to do their dirty work and make her let in gargoyles around RA, Tara is the one who takes the fall. Not them."

"Wait… Clarissa?" Raina sounds shocked. "She's an awful girl, but she's not a villain."

"Yeah, Devin, that's stretching it," Sasha agrees. "Clarissa is from a powerful royal family."

"I saw her introduce Tara to Princess Dragonfly, and she has been very vocal about how bad RA is without Olivina in charge," I point out. "And that day in the Rose Garden she was as cool as a cucumber and knew exactly how to escape the gargoyles through an unlocked window. I'm telling you, if Princess Dragonfly is in league with Olivina, so is Clarissa. She wants nothing more than to see RA go back to its old ways. And by Tara taking the fall in front of the royal court today, Olivina can pretend to stop Tara's attack and look like the hero."

"Kind of brilliant move if you ask me," Heath admits.

"Then let's get up there and stop her." I grab the sack of weapons I packed—a bow and arrow, a wand, a slingshot. (We didn't have time to get much of Prue and Corden's ultra-cool techy stuff.)

"So are we just going to walk in on a group of adult

JEN CALONITA

gargoyles ready to eat us?” Logan asks nervously. “Tell me
there is a secret passageway or *something*.”

Sasha holds up a bag. “You brought the strawberries and
I have the radishes. We can knock them out cold, then use
the strawberries…to do who-knows-what.”

“We’re going to have to improvise,” Heath says, shielding
his eyes and looking up at the fort high above us. “We’ve
faced villains before. We can do it again.”

“And end evil this time.” Sasha angrily stares up at the
tower. “This kingdom already got rid of two villains. We just
need to get rid of one more.”

“Hopefully the third time is the charm,” Raina says.
“Olivina beat us once, then we beat her with Tara’s help, so
maybe now we can do it on our own.”

“We can do this. We *have to*,” I stress. “And we start by reaching that window.” I point upward. *Charlie, could you drop us off?*

No problem! Charlie dips his head for me to climb aboard.

“Here’s what we’re going to do: we’ll climb aboard the
Pegasi two at a time and slip in that window,” I tell the others.
“Then what?”

“We can get the babies out of harm’s way and then find
Tara,” Heath says.

"Maybe they'll know something," Sasha adds.

"Raina and I will grab the babies," Logan says, sounding brave, and I gape. "Don't act so surprised. Keeping the babies safe is the quickest way out of the battle! We'll get out of there fast." He hands me the strawberries. "Here. You may need these."

I clutch the strawberries tight. "Let's go get our friends." Anna and I climb aboard Charlie and head straight for the tower, Charlie staying close to the wall as we ascend. I'm on edge, waiting for a gargoyle to appear and swoop down and grab us, but all is quiet as we reach the window ledge. Anna climbs in first.

"Coast is clear!" she whispers as she helps me inside. I hear all kind of squealing. "No one is here but the babies!"

Dimitri! Dimitri! Edgar sees us and waddles over, holding his hands up to me. I lift him up and see the other five babies in a large basket in the middle of the stone-walled room. There are a few bowls of water, but no food and the room is hot. Some of the babies look a bit sleepy from the heat.

"I'm so sorry, buddy," I say, not sure if he can understand me since I don't speak gargoyle like Anna does. I guess I'll have to learn. "I shouldn't have let her take you away."

He places his arms around my neck, seemingly no worse for wear. *Mean lady*, he tells me. *Girls. Girls crying! Have Mama!*

I can understand him perfectly. I know I'm not evil, and I realize now he's not either.

It makes me wonder how many other creatures are there out there in the kingdom that have gotten a bad rap just like the gargoyles? A good caretaker shouldn't judge. I make a silent vow to be better about this from now on.

"He says whoever has Tara is making her and Brynn cry," I tell the others and look at Anna. "I understood him."

Anna scoops up two more babies. "Me too," she says with a small smile.

"Pass the babies out the window!" Logan hisses as his Pegasus flaps his wings outside. Raina is seated behind him. "We can each hold three."

I hoist Edgar higher and bring him to the window. "Go with our friends," I tell him. "They'll keep you safe."

Mama? he asks, his eyes big and worried.

"We will find her," I promise. I think for a moment. I may not speak gargoyle yet, but Anna was able to communicate with Edgar. Maybe I can ask him some questions too. I try. "But Edgar, I need to know something: Why do we need strawberries?"

To help Mama! he says as I pass him out to Raina.

"How do they help Mama?" I say as Anna passes out two more babies.

BAM!

A giant gargoyle swoops in from the other window and knocks me to the floor with a massive wing.

"Devin!" Raina cries.

"Go!" I shout as the gargoyle makes its way back to me. "Save the babies!"

Anna reaches for the last two babies and runs back to the window, but Logan and Raina have already disappeared.

SCREECH!

I roll right before the gargoyle can land on me a second time. Anna holds the babies close, pushing them into a corner and blocking them as they start to wail.

Swish!

I hear something fly through the air and knock the gargoyle to the ground. It falls hard and is out cold. I look to the window in wonder.

Heath and Sasha are climbing through, and Heath has a slingshot.

"Pass me the babies!" Sasha cries as Heath fires another radish through the air.

Anna picks them up again and starts running.

"Look out!" she cries as two more gargoyles come flying through the other open window. Anna has no choice but to retreat to the corner again with the babies. The gargoyle turns toward them as the other comes for me.

We're trapped.

"Hang on!" I scream as I reach for my bow and arrow.

"Don't hurt them!" Anna shouts. "That's Beatrice's mom! She's obviously under a spell!"

"Trying, Anna!" I cry, as I use my bow to hit one on the head and roll out of the way. "But I don't want to get ripped apart either!"

Heath dives into the room and shoots two more radishes. They knock the gargoyles out, but I can still hear screeching in the distance.

"More are coming! We can't get the babies out by Pegasi," Sasha says. "It's too dangerous."

"Look! Stairs!" Anna says, pointing to a darkened corner of the tower. She heads toward them, one baby tucked securely under each arm.

"Go!" I tell the horse outside the window. "We'll call for you when we can."

"But what about Tara?" Sasha shouts as we tear off after Anna with Heath at my heels.

Thud!

Several more gargoyles are descending behind us as we take the stairs, running down into the darkness.

"Devin!" Heath cries and I spin around.

One gargoyle has Heath by the back of his jacket and is trying to drag him back up the staircase. I fumble for the bag of radishes and get bumped by Sasha running toward me. The radishes tumble out of the bag and down the stairs.

"No!"

I grab my slingshot from the bag at my waist, pull it out and grab a small stone from the floor, then fire it straight at the gargoyle's shoulder. The creature screeches and releases Heath. I grab my friend and pull him toward us. He's got a huge gash on his shoulder.

"I'm fine! Keep going!" he says, but his voice sounds off.

Down below, I see light and realize Anna and the babies must have reached the end of the stairs and gone out a door.

"There's a way out!" I shout to Sasha and Heath and bound ahead, breaking into the sunlight. I've barely taken a gulp when I feel myself pulled into the air. "*Aaah!*"

A gargoyle is lifting me high over the wall. When I look down, two others have Heath and Sasha. I don't see Anna or the babies anywhere. Logan and Raina have also disappeared.

My instinct is to kick out and get away, but we're too high up for me to drop. The wind whips my hair as we're flown to the other side of the crumbling fort, hovering over a half-built room overlooking Royal Court Manor. The gargoyle releases me from several feet up and I hit the ground hard.

I try to stand before it can grab me again. Heath and Sasha tumble down next to me and I hear Heath cry out, his arm already in tatters. A gargoyle lands on my back, pushing me down again. I can feel its claws cutting through the back of my dress.

"Hello, Devin."

I look up and see Princess Dragonfly walking toward me.

"I have to say, I'm surprised it took you so long to get here," she says. "I would have thought you'd catch on sooner to what I was doing, but then again, you did tell me exactly where to find Tara." She motions to the corner of the crumbling wall ledge, where I see Tara rocking back and forth, mumbling to herself as a gargoyle stands guard next to her.

I try to get up, and the gargoyle pushes me down again. "What did you do to her? What do you want?"

The princess laughs, the sound catching on the wind whooshing through the crumbling walls. Half a broken window overlooks the courtyard of Royal Court Manor, and I can see tiny specks moving about, unaware that gargoyles will soon attack the medal ceremony.

"Oh, I think you know that too. Power, of course." She leans down next to me. "Isn't that what every villain wants? Power and the chance to flaunt it? Oh, and to make someone else take the fall. You've helped me do that nicely. When these gargoyles descend on Royal Court Manor, it won't be long before Olivina swoops in to save the royal court and admits her granddaughter is the true villain behind these attacks."

"Tara wouldn't do that!" I cry. "You're controlling her. And where is Anna? Or Brynn?"

"Oh, the FTRS girl got away with those two babies just now, but she won't get far. As for that former lady-in-waiting of yours, well, I got tired of her trying to protect Tara, so I took care of her myself."

She snaps her fingers and Brynn floats out of the shadows, fast asleep.

"That spell should hold her for a while, just like these gargoyles should hold you till I find a way to dispose of you once and for all." Princess Dragonfly walks across the fort wall and kneels down by Tara. "Dear? It's time to work! Come, come, now! Let's tell these gargoyles where to go as you have before. They're completely in your hands, darling."

My head is spinning, but there is a persistent thought digging at me that I can't ignore. Princess Dragonfly's speech: *Darling? Dear? Dispose of us once and for all?* It's very familiar. And how would Princess Dragonfly know Brynn used to be my lady-in-waiting if she's a new teacher? I lift my head up again, pushing hard against the gargoyle to try to rise. Princess Dragonfly isn't *working* for Olivina—she *is* Olivina! "You're not Princess Dragonfly. You're the fairy godmother!" I shout.

"What?" Sasha looks at me.

Princess Dragonfly slowly turns around and laughs. "Good work, Devin! I was wondering when you'd figure that out. Took you longer than it should have."

"That's impossible!" Heath sputters.

"Nothing is impossible when you have skill, Heathcliff, dear." Princess Dragonfly waves her hand and produces a wand.

Waving it over herself, she spins around. I watch as the tiny, wiry woman disappears, replaced by the rotund, white-haired woman in a blue gown I remember with fear. "Surprise!"

"How? Why come back?" Sasha cries as I gape.

"You think I'm going to leave the kingdom I built from the ground up?" Her eyes flash. "Enchantasia is mine! That fool Rumpelstiltskin tried to steal it, but I knew he couldn't manage. You can't be outwardly evil. You have to act as if you're doing the kingdom a service. Saving the royal court from the gargoyles I'm sending to destroy them puts me in a position of power again. It makes me the hero of my own fairy tale!"

I try to think fast. I need to stall her. Make her stay longer. Maybe Anna, Logan, or Raina can reach the royal court and warn them. "How did you do it?" I ask.

"It was all so simple," Olivina says with a wicked gleam. "I disappeared into the deepest part of the Hollow Woods after you all tried to ruin me, but after the battle, when the schools were in tatters, I knew I had an opening to return. People are frightened. These subjects and even that blasted royal court I created will believe anything if they think you can save them. I just needed to find a way to put myself in the position of hero once more. When one of my trusted students sent word that

RA needed new teachers, I applied. I fudged my credentials, hexed a few people to make them believe I actually taught in Nottingham, and voilà! With a little help from inside RA, Tara was easy enough to continue to control."

"Help from Clarissa Hartwith?" I ask, and Olivina simply raises an eyebrow. "How dare you use a student like that," I seethe, struggling to get up. "Tara thought she was losing her mind!"

Olivina smiles wickedly. "You were the fool who made her come back. And now I'm here to stay."

"You won't get away with this!" Heath shouts.

"Oh, Heathcliff, I already have."

Olivina pulls Tara up to standing. "Go on now, dear. Tell the gargoyles where to go! It must be you, child. I can have no part of this." She marches Tara over to the crumbling window ledge and the gargoyles watch them.

Thud! I hear screeching and more banging around.

"Don't do it, Tara!" Sasha shouts.

"The others have arrived, darling! They're all waiting on your command!" she pushes. "Come along now!"

Tara stands at the window, her breath ragged as she stares out at Royal Court Manor.

"Raise your hand. Make the command," Olivina coos.

"Don't do it, Tara!" I cry. "Fight her!"

"I can't," Tara whispers to us.

"You can!" Heath insists. "Fight her!"

"*Now* Tara." Olivina's voice sharpens like a knife. "I'm growing impatient. I'll count you down. Five, four…"

"*Aaaah!*" Anna comes charging out of nowhere with a log and barrels into Olivina. It hits the fairy godmother and knocks her sideways. She grabs Tara and starts dragging her out of the room. "Devin!" she cries, making eye contact. "Grab the—"

Boom! Olivina zaps Anna with her wand, and the girl falls down flat.

"No!" I cry and Sasha shrieks.

Oh my fairies, is Anna dead? Is she stunned? She isn't moving. And where are the other two babies? What did Anna want me to grab? I look around wildly, but there is nothing on the fort wall I could use as a weapon. Just some crumbling rocks from the walls, and some old wood that might have once been a table. I lost my slingshot in the tower. I lost my bow and arrow. I have nothing left but… I feel my waist and the sack attached to it. All I have is a bag of strawberries. And I have no clue what they're for.

"Well, that was a bit surprising, but all is fine now." Olivina dusts herself off and practically drags Tara in front of the window. "Work your magic, child, so I can fly off and save the kingdom. Come along!"

"NO!" Tara shouts, sounding much stronger suddenly.

Olivina looks startled. "Don't make me charm you again, child. You've already had one too many charms." She tsks. "Any more and I fear it will destroy you. Do as your grandmother tells you now."

There still has to be a way to stop this. What if Anna meant the strawberries? What if they can do something none of us realize? What if the babies told her something that I could do? I reach down for the bag and pray the gargoyle doesn't see. I place my hand inside and grasp a single berry. I pull the berry out and *SCREECH*!

The gargoyle pins me down again and the strawberry rolls from my hand.

The gargoyle sniffs the strawberry, curious, then removes a hand from my back to pick it up and pop it in its mouth. Seconds later, it jumps off me in a daze, looking around.

What…what is happening to me? I hear it say. *Where is my baby? Where am I?* The gargoyle backs up, panicked.

I look at it in surprise. The strawberries are an antidote!

Olivina laughs. "Oh, Devin, you fool. Gargoyles are allergic to radishes! Not strawberries! Ridiculous girl. You'd never have made a good creature caretaker. I was clearly mistaken about your talents."

"Oh?" I reach my hand into the bag and toss a strawberry at both of the gargoyles holding Heath and Sasha. Immediately they let go of my friends and look around wildly.

Where are the babies? Where are we?

"What is going on?" Olivina says, looking mildly concerned.

I toss the bag to Heath. "Toss the other berries to those outside!" I cry. Heath looks at me strangely. "Hurry!" He does as he's told.

A gargoyle comes roaring toward me, screeching. *Where is my baby? How did I get here?*

I don't know if the gargoyles can understand me, but I have to try. "That woman put you under a spell and stole your babies. They're safe, but we have to stop her or she'll strike again! She's the one who tried to control you! Get her!"

Olivina starts to back up, but the three gargoyles in the room are heading straight toward her.

"No, no, now. Let's be sensible. We can make a deal!" she cries as one picks her up. "We can rule together!"

"Rule? You're no ruler," I say as they lift her up. "You don't even belong in this kingdom. Maybe it's time you finally left us all alone."

The mama gargoyle and I make eye contact as she lifts Olivina higher. Olivina's wand falls from her fingers.

"Wait!" she cries as a second gargoyle helps carry the fairy godmother away. "Wait!" she screams, but the gargoyles rise into the air and disappear into the clouds, carting her off. Soon, the famed fairy godmother is just a tiny speck in the sky. I can't help but hope that is the last time we ever see or hear of her.

Sasha races for Tara, who is still shaking, while I dive for Anna.

"Tara? Tara?" Sasha cries as Tara continues to mutter to herself. "Can you hear me? She's still under a spell!"

I shake Anna, but she still isn't moving. It's like she's in a deep trance, like Brynn, still hovering in the air behind us. Olivina's spells are still controlling them, I realize. But how do I break them with her no longer here? I spy the wand across the room and lunge for it. Without thinking, I snap it in half.

Anna sits up and gasps. Tara collapses against a wall, and Brynn starts to fall.

"Got her!" Heath says, arriving back in time to catch her in his arms.

"Oh my!" Brynn says. "What just happened? Where are we?"

"Olivina," Tara gasps through tears. "She had me. She's been controlling me. She's—"

"Gone now," Sasha says firmly. "And I suspect she'll *never* be heard from again."

Anna blinks twice as she clutches her chest, which I suspect must really hurt from that wand strike. "The strawberries?"

"They saved us," I tell her. "You are a hero."

Anna beams. "Well that's something I've never been called before." Then she reaches over and hugs me. And I actually let her.

Happily Ever After Scrolls

Brought to You by FairyWeb—Enchantasia's
Number One News Source

Royal Academy: The Revolution

by Sasha Briarwood

Well, we did it, royal watchers. Again.

We've stopped the kingdom of Enchantasia from another villain. (Maybe I need to change my career from journalist to protector of the kingdom.)

What many in the kingdom have been talking about all week can finally be confirmed: Olivina, the former headmistress of Royal Academy who was ousted for her wicked ways, was secretly plotting to take over the kingdom again. Poising as a new teacher at Royal Academy and with help from a small group of loyal students, Olivina attempted to bewitch her granddaughter, Tara, and cause a gargoyle uprising that would destroy our royal court and send fear and panic throughout the kingdom.

"Her plan was to look like the hero of the fairy tale when she was actually the puppetmaster of our story, pulling all the strings," says Headmaster Pierce. "Thankfully, some of our students—and a Fairy Tale Reform School student—stopped her." That FTRS student was none other than Gilly Cobbler's younger sister, Anna Cobbler. (Yes, the same Anna who almost destroyed this kingdom during the Battle of Rumpelstiltskin. See that, readers? People *can* change!)

And speaking of change, this kingdom needs to change their opinion of gargoyles as well. It turns out they have been misunderstood. As the gargoyles told the royal court during a closed session with translators Anna Cobbler and Devin Nile (who are both studying to be magical creature caretakers), they were long controlled by Rumpelstiltskin and Alva. When the Battle of Rumpelstiltskin ended, their spell was broken. Realizing what they'd done to help the villain, they went into hiding with their babies. Then Olivina came calling and figured out how to control them for her own nefarious purposes. Now they're finally free.

"The gargoyles asked to be observed for a while, so we gave them their own property on Fairy Tale Reform School grounds, where they can live for however long they like," says Professor Harlow of Fairy Tale Reform School.

The gargoyles have invited students and subjects to visit them on their grounds so that they can see firsthand how harmless these creatures actually are. Bonus: Visitors will also get to observe a new crop of gargoyles babies who, this reporter can personally attest, are pretty darn cute.

◇◇◇◇◇◇◇◇

Stay tuned for more on the new dawn of Enchantasia in this column and in Sasha Briarwood's own blog, the Enchantasia Insider.

PASSING THE TORCH

As I watch the gargoyles frolicking in a waterfall and sitting atop stone pillar perches on their new protected land, I can tell they're happier than I've ever seen them. Edgar is taking a bath in the fountain and squirting water everywhere and laughing. He sees me and waves.

Dimitri! he says and I wave right back.

"I think you're his favorite," Anna says as she walks up alongside me wearing her Fairy Tale Reform School uniform.

"Hmm…debatable," I say. "I think they all like you best."

Anna grins. "Tied for first?"

I smile. "Deal."

"So…I heard a rumor," Anna says and side-eyes me. "Is it true you're leaving school?"

I nod, feeling suddenly nervous again. "That's the plan. I mean, my parents are coming this afternoon to have a discussion about it, but my dad promised if we stopped Olivina and it was safe, I could go to Nottingham." Anna's face falls. "Is something wrong?" I ask.

"I'm going to kind of miss having you around," she admits. "I know we didn't get along at first, but no one knows magical creature caretaking like you do." Her brown eyes are wide. "How am I going to learn without you here to teach me?"

"I'm sure Snow and Pierce will bring back more classes soon, and Snow is the best teacher around," I remind her. "You're going to learn plenty! You already know how to speak gargoyle so you're going to be way beyond most kids in class."

Anna still looks worried. "But no one else in class wants to be a magical creature caretaker like we do, probably. They're just taking the class for fun. You're the only one who truly understands me."

I smile. I know the feeling better than Anna realizes. "So then we'll write. I'm only a Pegasus Post away! And I can even send you books from school—if I get to go. Maybe someday you'll get to go there too." I picture myself sending Anna stuff from Nottingham and smile. Sometimes you just need a push. Brynn admitted she was the one who sent me that first school brochure, not realizing it could cause concern with Snow. "I just knew it was somewhere you needed to be, just like I knew I always belonged at RA," she told me. Brynn was so right.

"You're going," Anna says resolutely. "I can feel it."

"I hope so," I say as I look at the gargoyles again. "And this isn't goodbye. After I'm trained in Nottingham and you're trained up here, we'll team up together again."

"Really?" Anna beams. "I'd like that."

I hear a commotion nearby and see two small boys come racing toward the gargoyles' watering hole. One starts to climb the fence.

"Han, no!" Anna cries and swoops in to pull him down. "You too, Hamish." A girl comes running, followed by her parents and an older girl. "Oh, you're here!" Anna says excitedly. "Devin, before you go, you have to meet my family. This is my mother, my father, my twin brothers, my sister Trixie, and this is my sister Gilly. My brother Felix is visiting our Grandma Pearl, but everyone else wanted to meet you."

Gilly and I look at each other in wonder.

"Hey…" I start to say. Gilly looks familiar. Suddenly, I remember this time when I went with Mother to the bakery in Enchantasia Village a few years back. "Aren't you the girl who…"

She points at me. "You're the one with the bracelet," she says. "From the bakery."

"Yes," I say, remembering.

"Yes," she says, clearly picturing the same moment when we met. I haven't run into her since. I never realized *the* girl was the girl who saved the kingdom. If she had said her name then, I don't recall. So *this* is Gilly Cobbler.

"You two know each other?" Anna says in wonder.

"Sort of," Gilly says with a cock of her head. "So you're Devin Nile, the one my sister keeps talking about. Nice to officially meet you."

"You too," I say and we just smile.

"*Anna!*" one of the younger boys whines. "You promised you'd show us the sanctuary and let us talk to the gargoyles."

"Be right there! I should go," Anna says to me apologetically.

"Before you go, I wanted to give you something." I reach into the sack I was carrying and produce my magical creature caretaker kit. "I heard everyone gets a kit at Nottingham so I won't be needing mine."

"I couldn't," Anna says as she takes the bag from me anyway. "I mean, really?"

"Yes!" I say. "Someone has to give the animals of this kingdom good medical care while I'm gone." I pat the bag in her arms. "I know you'll do me proud."

"Thanks, Devin!" Anna says and hugs me for the second time this week. "I'll send you updates all the time!" she promises. And then she's off and running to talk to her family.

I have a feeling the creatures in this kingdom are going to be in good hands.

NEW BEGINNINGS

You're sure you're sure about this? Like really sure? Like a hundred percent sure?" my mother asks a short time later in the headmasters' office.

"Dear, we did promise her," Father says and smiles at me. "She really wants this."

"I do," I swear. "I really do. I think I belong there."

"But you won't be properly royally trained or part of any of the redevelopment of this kingdom," Mother reminds me. "The royals will be out in full force now, showing the kingdom how safe we are and how we're rebuilding. Emerson worked so hard to have you be a part of her Operation Royal Refresh."

"I think Emerson will be fine without Devin," Headmaster

Pierce says gently on my behalf. "She has plenty of students to utilize, while your daughter would be better served by a school that specifically focuses on what she was born to do—magical creature caretaking."

"I've never met someone so skilled at this," Headmistress Snow seconds. "Devin was born for this role. If it weren't for her and Anna Cobbler, we'd still be hunting for Olivina and convinced gargoyles were to blame. Devin and Anna have changed the course of history. Anyone who does that doesn't need a royal title to shine."

"Probably not," Mother agrees with a sigh. She looks at me. "I just wanted you to be the perfect princess, but I guess being a caretaker doesn't mean you're not."

I grab my mother's hand. "I think you and I both know I was born for something different. Having a title has always weighed me down," I say and sneak a peek at Pierce, who told me the same thing once. "I need to spread my wings and see what I can do with my gift. When I'm done training, I promise you, I'll come back to Enchantasia and share my gift with this kingdom that I truly love."

Mother sobs. "I just want you to be happy."

"I already am," I say and hug her. "This is what I want."

Mother pulls back and looks at me with tears in her eyes. She's stopped sobbing. "Then go fly, Devinaria Nile."

That's exactly what I prepare to do.

After Snow calls Nottingham, which agrees to accept me as a transfer after I've finished my paperwork, and I sign all my transfer scrolls, Father, Mother, and I emerge from their offices. Pierce and Snow both make me promise to stay in touch and keep them posted. I'm welcome back anytime, and I promise to visit. I could never stay away from Enchantasia forever.

"But what about my Operation Royal Refresh!" protests Emerson when we share the news. "Who will be a good spokesperson for RA?"

"About that…" I open the office door. Brynn is waiting with a stack of scrolls. "I think I have the perfect replacement for me."

"Hi, Emerson!" Brynn says cheerily. "I've been doing some research on royals throughout the realms, and I really think we could benefit from more outreach activities throughout the kingdom. Meet and greets are so overdone, but some charity work and some rebuilding projects done with students and the locals will really put the students at RA in a good light."

"That *is* a good idea," Emerson says in surprise. "What else do you have?"

The two wander off talking and I smile. I can't wait to see how Brynn shapes this school and this kingdom.

"So we'll be back at the end of the week to get you and all your things," Father is telling me as Mother hugs me goodbye. "And we'll personally bring you to Nottingham ourselves."

"You will?" I say in surprise.

"Of course!" Mother says. "I want to see this school that's so much better than RA. And maybe a real dragon, up close. As a child, I used to pretend I had an imaginary pet dragon, and I used to talk to it."

"You did?" I say in surprise.

Mothers winks. "I did. I guess we're not as different as I thought."

"*Ridiculous!* I mean, the nerve of this school! Getting rid of footmen and ladies-in-waiting," we hear someone yelling. I look down the hall to see a man and a woman dragging a trunk. Clarissa is walking sullenly behind them. It's the Hartwiths.

"We'll let you go," Mother says. "I don't want to get stuck talking to those people." She kisses my cheek and is gone.

The Hartwiths travel past me without a word, but Clarissa stops long enough to give me a nasty look.

"Leaving, Clarissa?" I ask pleasantly.

"I hope you're happy with what you've done," she snaps. "Because of you, I've been expelled! Not banished, but expelled! Me and my entire group of friends. Father says they can't prove anything, but our name is now mud. We're going to have to move to Wonderland to get way from the stink you put on my family."

I step closer and smile. "You mean the stink *you* put on your family. Siding with a villain will always bring you down in the end. I hope it was worth it."

She turns her nose up and walks away, trailing her parents and her trunk.

I breathe a sigh of relief. Royal Academy is better off already.

"Well, it's official!" I say, bounding up to my friends to tell them all about my conversation with my parents and the headmasters (and what happened with Clarissa). "I'm a Nottingham student now." The group cheers.

"Are you sure about this?" Prue asks as Corden looks on worriedly. "Things are changing here for real now."

"Yes." Tara's voice is firm, and I notice she's wearing her

Royal Academy students' sash and pin. "And we need all the strong royals we can get to make sure it stays that way. We could use someone like you to help keep villains at bay."

"I suspect you all have things covered," I tell them. "And if anything gets out of hand, call for me. I'm only a post away."

"You better be staying for supper at least," Logan tells me. "I helped cook tonight and we're having roast duck that I marinated for days in your honor." He blanches. "Except I forgot you're a vegetarian. Fiddlesticks." We all laugh.

"I'm staying till the end of the week so you'll have plenty of time to cook me some great meals."

"On it!" Logan says.

"I'm going to really miss you, roomie," Sasha says, looping an arm through mine.

"I am going to miss you too," I admit. "But everyone has to figure out where they truly belong, and I belong at the Nottingham School for Nature and Wild Beasts. I will be back. You have my word."

I look at my friends. I never thought I'd have such good ones when I used to wander around the woods all day talking to animals. They've changed me. Our battles have changed me. And I know we all will continue to grow. More than anything, I know this isn't the end of our story. "We'll all be back together someday," I promise. Raina sniffs. "And I expect you all to write! And visit!"

Logan looks at me worriedly. "Only if they don't have dragons."

"I'll protect you," Heath tells him. "But hey. Since you aren't going till the end of the week, how about another Pegasus flight? Now that we can use the stables again, and we've already flown on those guys, I'm itching to get back up in the air again."

"I'd love to," I say.

A few minutes later, Heath and I are off to the stables and saddling up.

"We're going to really miss you, blondie," he says as he climbs aboard. "Don't stay away too long. Okay?"

I climb aboard Charlie and smile. "Never. I'm not sure I can trust you to be on your own for too long. Who knows what kind of trouble you'd get into without me here to keep you in line."

"Very funny," he says and whistles to his horse. "And just for that, I'm going to race you. Loser has to buy the winner a Charmiccino." And he's off.

"Get him, Charlie!" I say with a laugh, and the Pegasus starts to gallop and race past the fields. I can see Heath just ahead of us as Charlie opens his wings wide and begins to soar up, up, up over Enchantasia and straight on to the Hollow Woods, and I can't help but smile. Win or lose today, I know I've already won. My life is just the way I always wanted it to be. So I just hold on tight, thankful that I finally know where this princess belongs.

"Speech! Speech!"

A Fairy Tale Reform School Bonus Story

OFFICIAL ENCHANTASIA CORRESPONDENCE FROM
Princesses Ella, Rapunzel, Rose & Snow

Dear Gillian Cobbler of 2 Boot Way,

Your presence has been requested at the Royal Court this coming Thursday to receive the:

Magical Medal of Honor

for bravery shown during the Battle of Rumpelstiltskin and your unfailing devotion to the kingdom of Enchantasia.

Your parents and siblings are invited to attend this prestigious ceremony with you.* Refreshments and light snacks will be served.

TIME: 4:00 P.M.

*Due to the current threat level in the kingdom, only named guests and immediate family will be permitted to attend. Please arrive thirty minutes prior for Dwarf Squad briefings. No wands, magical artifacts, or ogre bodyguards will be allowed into the Royal Court.

I'm not going to lie. This has been a doozy of a week.

Rumpelstiltskin and Alva placed a curse on the kingdom and almost wiped Enchantasia from existence. My boot was destroyed, but it was rebuilt just like my school. My younger sister Anna surprisingly went from villain sidekick to newly minted FTRS student. And somehow, in the middle of all that, I got this letter saying I'm receiving the Magical Medal of Honor.

"Do you understand how prestigious this award is?" Mother asks as she holds the thick, cream-colored invitation in her shaking hands. "This award has only been given out once before to Red Riding Hood! And now it's going to you!"

"*And* Gilly's friends," Trixie adds as she turns the purple velvet box the invite arrived in into a bed for one of her dolls. "Jax, Ollie, Kayla, Jocelyn, Maxine, and Allison Grace are getting it too, I'm sure."

"Absolutely!" Father booms, looking at the invite over Mother's shoulder. With him here, the room now smells like a mix of shoe leather and polish. (Mother screamed so loud when the royal guards showed up with this proclamation that he came running from his newly rebuilt cobbler shop in the boot's heel.) "It's nice to see the royals recognize all you and your friends have done to help Enchantasia." Father claps a hand on my shoulder. "I'm very proud of you, Gillian."

"Thank you, Father," I say, blushing slightly. I still haven't gotten used to Father's compliments. As a former thief, I still have a hard time accepting the world sees me not just as a reformed FTRS student, but a hero. And a part-fairy one at that.

For the love of Grimm, that is going to take some getting used to.

"And we're invited to watch the ceremony!" My brother Han shouts with excitement as Hamish does a jig behind him. Felix is the only one who will miss party. He's been staying with Grandma Pearl on her island ever since the curse to get some well-needed rest and relaxation (the Stiltskin Squad breaking into our boot really did a number on him.) He's loving the island though, and cooking lessons from Grandma Pearl, who, according to his last Pegasus Post, can make a mean streusel. Mother said we can all go visit them on our next school break.

Yes, I actually have school breaks again! Now that Professor Sebastian has transitioned my friends and me to the Magical Metamorphosis Fairy Tale Reform School Day Program, we get weekends home and school vacations again. After all the villain dealings the past few months, I have to say I don't mind quiet evenings helping Father sew shoes when I'm not playing Duck Duck Goose with my siblings. Post-curse, FTRS is a bit of a mess anyway. Turns out the golden egg was able to reverse part of the school damage, but the whole castle has to be inspected by the Royal Court and the ELF Construction Crew for charms/hexes/curses before classes can be held in certain wings again. I've had to do a lot of our class work via mini magical scrolls. Speaking of which...

"Mother, I have to tap into my scroll for class," I say,

heading to the stairs leading to the newly reconstructed loft. It is a lot roomier than our old one! After our boot was badly damaged by the Stiltskin Squad, our village was so grateful for our family's help in stopping the curse that they got together to help build us a bigger, better boot on the same plot of land. It only took a few weeks to magically put up. Turns out when the Royal Court gives their blessing, and you don't have to deal with the ELF Construction Crew, things move quickly. The heel where Father has his cobbler shop is twice the size of our old one, and the upper part of our boot has three bedrooms instead of one. For the first time, my siblings and I don't have to share a bed. Trixie and I are rooming together on weekends in a triple bunk bed with room for Anna when she finally reforms and leaves FTRS. I fear it might be a while though. To be supportive, I wrote her a Pegasus Post last week with lots of FTRS tips (avoid Professor Harlow before she's had her coffee, learn to duck and roll to make it through moving doorways, and make sure you get sentenced to detention at least once to see Madame Cleo's fish tank–like classroom, which is too cool to be believed).

"Gillian, the ceremony is in three days!" Mother calls to me. "We need to discuss what you're wearing."

"My school uniform," I say automatically and there is silence. I look back and see Mother and Father frowning. Even Trixie looks perturbed. "What's wrong with my uniform?"

"Nothing…it's just…didn't Professor Sebastian say it isn't required of you anymore? You can wear anything you want as long as it's appropriate for a big, fancy ceremony." Mother taps her chin. "And you know, glass slippers from your father would certainly be appropriate."

Father's eyes light up. "That's true. I've never made you a pair."

I burst out laughing. Glass slippers? For me? "*Mother*," I say, my voice sounding almost villainous, "I'm not wearing a ballgown or uncomfortable shoes. We've talked about this."

"Don't call your father's shoes uncomfortable! I'm just asking you to dress up this one time. Gillian, the artists who do portraits at this event will capture this moment for all fairy tale time! You can't wear that blue dress again. Every portrait I've seen of you is in that dress."

"Because it's my uniform!" I counter. "And I'm used to wearing it." Even now that I'm home for the weekend I have it on. "This blue dress and the striped stockings are a part of me. I can't imagine life without them or my friends from school." The mini magical scroll in my hand starts to chime, and I climb the stairs faster. "We will talk about this later!"

Reaching the landing, I rush into the girls' room and climb up to the top bunk to take the scroll call. It's a new feature added with the help of Professor Harlow's magic, to aid in studies during the curse aftermath. (My friends and I have secretly been using it to chat, but I haven't told my parents that part.)

I tap the scroll with my wand and it starts to glow and waffle. Suddenly I see a bunch of images. The little heads of Jocelyn, AG, Jax, Ollie, and Kayla appear in glowing boxes along with Maxine's right arm. Across the top of the mirror-like screen is a small pocket watch with a countdown clock. We have ten minutes.

"You guys there?" Maxine shouts. "I can't see anyone! Hello?" WHACK! WHACK! She hits the screen with her wand. "Is this thing on?"

"Maxine!" Jocelyn says in a drawl that sounds eerily like her big sister, the Evil Queen. "We told you a thousand times—you have to back up! You're too big to fit on the magical scroll if you stand too close."

"Well, not a *thousand* times," Ollie interjects. "We've only done this five times. But you get the point, right, Maxine?"

There's the sound of shuffling, quacking, and something crashing to the ground.

"Peaches, no!" we hear Maxine shout. "You can't eat my scroll. We've talked about this! We'll go for a swim after the call!" More quacking. "Peaches, just be a good duck and talk to everyone."

A beak appears in Maxine's frame. *QUACK!*

"Peaches, not so loud!" AG groans.

Suddenly, Maxine's toothy ogre grin appears in her small box. A puddle of drool slips from her mouth. "There you all are! Hi! Sorry about Peaches. She gets jealous. Can you hear me?" WHACK! WHACK! "Is this working?"

"YES!" we all shout.

"Maxine, you're wasting time," AG says from the comfort of what looks like a canopy bed stacked with pillows. She must be in her parents' pop-up castle. There's even a pillow that looks like Professor Sebastian when he gets all beasty. I'm sure he likes that a ton. "We only have eight minutes now. We have to focus."

"Sorry," Maxine says. "I'm just so excited! Did you all get your invitations?"

"Are you kidding? Raz hasn't stopped talking about it," Jax says, referring to his famous sister, Rapunzel. "Or asking what I'm wearing. I'm *not* wearing royal threads. I'm doing my uniform, of course."

"Thank you!" I shout, my voice a bit loud.

"That's what I said too," Kayla chimes in. "My mother and sisters wanted to make me a fairy gown, but I like my uniform. It's very me."

"You're all batty," Jocelyn says with a snort. "Why would I wear my uniform to a ceremony where they're rewarding the Evil Queen's younger sister the Magical Medal of Honor? I'm whipping up something original." Her right hand starts to spark.

"Um, you never wear your uniform anyway, so this isn't really surprising," I point out.

Jocelyn's glowing face is eerily happily. "I'm an individual, Gilly. I can't wait for the world to get a load of what I come up with."

"*Anyway*," Ollie interrupts, "the reason I called for this mini magical scroll meeting was—"

"Wait," Maxine butts in. "This is a class call, isn't it? That's what my scroll flashed when the scroll call alert came up." She clears her throat and Peaches quacks again.

"That's so Professor Sebastian doesn't realize we're using the feature for our own devices," Jax says cheerily. "Don't you see? We've beat the system."

"Oh no." Maxine frowns. "That's not right."

"It's fine! We're not plotting to overthrow the Royal Court or anything," Jocelyn says. "We're just talking."

"*Privately.* If my dad caught wind we were using this new magical system just to chat, he'd flip," says AG with a nervous laugh. "That's why we have to keep all scroll calls under ten minutes so he doesn't get an alert on his scroll."

"Right," I agree. "So down to business. When we get the award—"

"Award!" Maxine jumps in again. "Can you believe it? Us getting an award. It's almost like getting a gold star on a paper." She sighs happily. "I've never gotten one, but I've always wanted to see that shiny gold star on one of my scrolls. I'd cut it out and make a pin out of it." Peaches quacks loudly. "No, you can't eat my award. Peaches, what did I say about eating my things? I don't even have the star yet and you're trying to eat it!"

"Maxine, please focus!" I beg.

"Sorry," Maxine says contritely.

"Seven minutes!" AG calls out.

"Now I assume they want some sort of speech," I try again, but there are groans all around. "Hey, don't think I'm excited about this either. AG or Jax, can you speak on our behalf? You guys are used to this sort of thing."

"No. Way," AG says. "I'd panic and start to transform right there at the podium."

"And I try to avoid speaking in front of *Happily Ever After Scrolls* as much as possible since they started referring to me as Jax of All Trades." He shudders. "I hate that nickname."

"I could do it!" Ollie volunteers. "We all know I'm good with a crowd."

"When you're doing magic tricks!" Jocelyn counters.

"What if I made the room disappear?" Ollie suggests. "Or did some ventriloquism? You know, I could easily get a parrot and—"

"No!" we all chorus.

"Anyone else? Anyone?" Jocelyn asks, but there is suddenly the sound of silence.

It's so quiet I can hear Han and Hamish singing "Twinkle Twinkle" downstairs. "Well, someone has to speak!" I say, and everyone is still quiet. "And it's not going to be me!"

"Come on, Gilly. You're the perfect spokesperson," Kayla says meekly.

"Everyone knows who you are," AG agrees. "You're like face of the curse. Er, I mean, anti-curse? Curse stopper?"

"I vote for curse killer," Ollie pipes up.

"I'll do it if Gilly won't!" Maxine waves her hands wildly in front of the frame as if we can't see her. "I love speaking to new people."

"Yes, but you always say too much, Maxine," Ollie reminds her. "You go on and on and tell all our secrets."

QUACK! QUACK! QUACK!

"Peaches, don't agree with him!" Maxine protests. "I only told Mother about you eating her favorite lamp after she accused a troll of breaking into our tree and taking it, which wasn't true." Peaches burps in response.

"I'm with Peaches," Jax says. "Maxine, I love ya, but you tend to run your mouth."

"Fine." Maxine hangs her head and drool spills onto Peaches head. "But just so you know, I was going to say some really nice things. I've been thinking about the speech ever since we got that invitation, and I really think…"

"We could all say something," AG interrupts. "Together,

maybe? That would be nice, since we all worked together to stop the curse and Rumpelstiltskin."

"Just hearing his name makes me twitch," Kayla says.

"I know," Jocelyn agrees quietly. "But he's gone now so… we should celebrate, right?"

"Right," Jax agrees, but he sounds hesitant. "That's what the Royal Court wants us to do but…"

"It's kind of scary to think of him being out there somewhere," Ollie says softly. "Like what if he comes back?" No one says anything for a moment.

"He's gone," AG says firmly, but I see her chin waffle. "Right?"

"Well…" Maxine starts to say.

"You never know," Kayla says. "What if he finds a way back to this realm? Or Alva does? Then what do they do? They're going to come after us first for sure."

"You think so?" Jax says.

"I'd think they'd just try to do the curse again and get it right this time," I ponder, trying not to be sick at the thought.

"If I was a villain you destroyed and I came back, I would hunt you all down," Jocelyn says matter-of-factly.

"Nice, Joc. Real nice!" Kayla snaps.

QUACK! QUACK! QUACK!

"Peaches! That's not nice to say," Maxine says. "But guys?"

"Hey, I'm being honest! I'm always honest!" Jocelyn insists.

"Yeah, but that doesn't mean we want your honesty all the time," AG says. "You're freaking us out."

"Yeah, not cool," Ollie agrees. "Maybe I should hire one of those ogre bodyguards advertising in *Happily Ever After Scrolls*."

"I saw that," Kayla says. "I told my mother she needs one, but she says we don't."

"Guys?" Maxine tries again.

"Would still be cool, wouldn't it?" Ollie says. "I'd love to say, 'Have you met my bodyguard?'"

"You don't need a bodyguard! Just be prepared for another attack," Jocelyn says.

"Isn't it a little soon to be so pessimistic?" I counter.

"GUYS!" Maxine's voice makes us all jump. "Can we all stop talking about what could happen and focus on what's happening right now? We're safe, and part of the reason this whole kingdom still exists is because of us. But if we're going to continue to be safe, we need every citizen and every creature in this kingdom to do their part and look out for one another. It's only when we work together—like we did for the curse—that we truly succeed, you know? We're a family, and even though families fight and disagree sometimes, they come together when it counts. We have each other's backs and we'll always have Enchantasia's as well. So while we may be getting this Magical Medal of Honor, it really belongs to everyone in this kingdom for doing what they could to stand up against evil. Because when we do that, we all win."

Everyone is stunned into silence

I clear my throat. "Wow, Maxine, that was really go—"

The roar that interrupts our conversation is so loud I practically fall off the bunk bed.

Professor Sebastian appears in AG's frame and starts to morph into his beastly half almost immediately. "ARE YOU ALL REALLY USING YOUR MINI MAGICAL SCROLLS TO HAVE A PRIVATE DISCUSSION?"

I can hear Beauty and AG in the background trying to calm him down. I'm too freaked out to speak.

"Maybe?" Ollie squeaks.

"All of you, off this scroll call NOW," Professor Sebastian says as Beauty's hand appears in the frame with a goblet of water. "Before I think of three detention essays to give each of you."

"But we're just trying to come up with a good speech," AG squeaks.

"You want a good speech?" he roars again. "Speak from the heart! Don't think. Just speak your mind. Be grateful. NOW OFF THIS SCROLL."

I go to tap my wand on the scroll when I hear the professor speak again.

"WAIT! STOP! Don't go yet." He's breathing hard.

"Really?" Ollie asks. "Did you want to hear my thoughts on ogre bodyguards?"

"NO!" Professor Sebastian barks. "What I wanted to say is to Maxine."

"Me?" Maxine's left eye starts to roll around in its socket. "I, um, I…" Peaches starts quacking again. "I'm really sorry, Professor."

"Sorry? You're the one who shouldn't be sorry!" he says. "I heard this whole conversation—I've heard several of your conversations actually…"

"Fairy be," I hear Kayla say under her breath.

"And if anyone is giving a speech at this Magical Medal of Honor ceremony, it's going to be Maxine and Maxine alone."

"Me?" Maxine says again, one of her eyeballs rolling faster.

"Yes, you! Your speech was perfect!" he says gruffly. "None of your classmates could say it better. Believe me."

"Ouch," Ollie whispers.

"Maxine?" Professor Sebastian speaks up. "Gold star for you."

"Really? YES!" Maxine hugs Peaches to her chest.

Professor Sebastian smiles.

"Go Maxine!" I cheer.

The rest of us start to clap and Jax whistles. Maxine's eyeball stops rolling and she grins toothily.

"Maxine! Maxine! Maxine!" Ollie chants and we all join in.

"ALL RIGHT! That's enough celebrating!" Professor Sebastian grunts, but I can see he's pleased. "No more magical scroll calls without permission. You hear me?"

"Yes, sir," we all agree.

"Goodnight!" His and AG's mini scroll screen goes dark.

There's only twenty seconds left on the pocket watch timer anyway. One by one the rest of the screens cut out till it's only me and Maxine left. I'm not ready to say goodbye yet. I miss my friends when I'm not with them. Maxine must feel the same way as she's still here, hugging Peaches and looking sort of misty.

"My first gold star, Gilly," she says dreamily.

I smile at my friend. "I'm sure it won't be your last," I say as we stare at each other till the pocket watch counts down, and poof! Our call ends. For tonight anyway.

Who are we kidding? Professor Sebastian threat or not, we'll still all be back on tomorrow.

ACKNOWLEDGMENTS

I was lucky enough to have two editors shepherd this book series to completion. Kate Prosswimmer was my partner-in-crime in kicking off Royal Academy Rebels, while Molly Cusick picked up the baton and went running to help me figure out *Outlaws* and *Heroes*. Editing an arc already in motion is tricky, and I'm so grateful Molly helped these rebels turned heroes have an epic adventure they could be proud of.

Writing the story is only the beginning of a book's journey, which is why I'm so thankful to the team at Sourcebooks, who sees to it that the Royal Academy Rebels are known far and wide. Thank you to Dominique Raccah for always supporting my stories, and Steve Geck, Margaret Coffee, Beth Oleniczak, Katie Stutz, Heather Moore, Lizzie Lewandowski, and Cassie Gutman, for seeing to it that the Royal Academy Rebels books truly shine. A special thanks to Mike Heath, who continues to blow me away with his covers. I think *Heroes* might be my favorite one yet!

Dan Mandel, thanks for being my light in the harbor (especially during a year like 2020). I'd be lost without you on this writing journey. I'm so lucky to have you as my agent.

The middle-grade and YA community stepped up this year in ways I could never imagine. I'm so thankful I can call (and Zoom!) with Elizabeth Eulberg, Kieran Scott, Courtney Sheinmel, Katie Sise, Sarah Mlynowski, Julie Buxbaum, Julia Devillers, Lindsay Currie, Tiffany Schmidt, and extraordinary library friends Rose Brock, Kelly Rechsteiner and JoBeth Roberts.

To my family, who has spent more time together this year than we ever thought possible, thank you for letting me hide in sections of the house to get my writing done and for putting up with my endless questions about lighting techniques, filming, and all the other ways we've tried to share our work via social media this year from our living room. Mike, Tyler, and Dylan, you are the best cheerleaders a girl could ask for.

Finally, to my readers: Nothing makes me happier than

hearing from you! Whether it's a note, an email, or a virtual visit, I feel so blessed to meet you and share this fairy-tale adventure with you. Thank you for coming on this journey with me.

ABOUT THE AUTHOR

Jen Calonita is the author of the Fairy Tale Reform School series, the Royal Academy Rebels series, and other books like *Secrets of My Hollywood Life* and *Turn It Up*. She rules Long Island, New York, with her husband, Mike; princes Tyler and Dylan; and their Chihuahuas, Captain Jack

© APRIL MERSINGER PHOTOGRAPHY

Sparrow and Ben Kenobi. The only castle she'd ever want to live in is Cinderella's at Walt Disney World. She'd love for you to visit her at jencalonitaonline.com and on Twitter @JenCalonita.

FAIRY TALE REFORM SCHOOL

EXPLORE MORE OF ENCHANTASIA IN THE ACCLAIMED SERIES THAT STARTED IT ALL!

Gilly Cobbler wouldn't call herself wicked, exactly…but when you have five little siblings and live in a run-down boot, you have to get creative to make ends meet. Gilly's a pretty good thief. *Until she gets caught.*

Gilly is sentenced to Fairy Tale Reform School, where all of the teachers are former villains, like the Big Bad Wolf and Cinderella's Wicked Stepmother. There's a battle brewing, and Gilly has to wonder: Can a villain really change?